SAVING MIA

ANNA STONE

© 2023 Anna Stone

All rights reserved. No part of this publication may be replicated, reproduced, or redistributed in any form without the prior written consent of the publisher.

This is a work of fiction. Names, characters, places, and incidents either are the products of the author's imagination or are used fictitiously. Any resemblance to actual persons, living or dead, businesses, companies, events, or locales is entirely coincidental.

ISBN: 9781922685094

CHAPTER 1

Cassandra was minutes away from closing the biggest deal of her career, and the only thing on her mind was *seduction*.

She kept her face stone as she listened to the dark-haired man at the other side of the conference room table drone on about cash flow and revenue. Henry Harris, the owner of Harris Industries, and what was soon to be her company's latest acquisition.

"As you can see," Henry continued, "Harris Industries has a history of delivering strong profits to our shareholders..."

Aside from in the past five years? That was when Henry inherited the family company. And because of his mismanagement, it was now millions of dollars in the red. It was doomed to go under.

Unless someone else acquired it. Someone who could turn it around. That was what Cassandra's firm did. And as CEO, acquisitions were her specialty.

So why was she thinking about seduction at a time like this? It wasn't the painfully dull conversation. And it certainly wasn't the company. Henry and the four men sitting at either side of him, all identical in shiny black shoes and Italian suits that couldn't hide the way their bellies hung over too-tight waistbands, were not the kind of people to inspire such feelings. And that was ignoring the fact that they were men. Men had never been on Cassandra's radar.

No, the reason seduction was on her mind was because it was just like a business deal.

First came the dance, the game of luring the other party in with flattery and hints of all the tantalizing rewards to come. Then came the overture, the proposition, either direct or indirect. Then the negotiation, the back and forth, the push and pull.

For the Harris acquisition, this had all taken place over the past few months, but she'd been laying the groundwork for almost a year. The time had come to seal the deal.

Because the pleasantries? The games? While Cassandra tolerated them as a means to an end, she preferred to get right down to business.

Across from her, Henry cleared his throat. "Miss Lee—"

"*Ms.*," Cassandra said.

"I beg your pardon?"

"*Ms.* Lee."

"Er, yes. Ms. Lee, what you're offering us is, frankly, insulting. We're not some fledgling startup. Harris Industries is an institution. We've been leaders in the field for generations. You must consider the potential profits..."

Cassandra allowed him to continue. But nothing he

could say would sway her. She already knew the outcome of their meeting.

She'd seen the numbers. And she could smell the desperation on him, hanging thick in the air like cologne. She'd known from the moment she walked into the conference room that she'd walk out of it victorious, a new acquisition under her belt.

And while Henry would never admit it, he knew it, too. But she indulged him. She allowed him to feel like he had some control over the situation. She allowed him to think he still held some power.

Were these games she played as CEO any different from sex? Running her own multi-billion-dollar company meant holding the kind of power and influence akin to that of monarchs of old. Wielding that kind of power meant always being in control.

And Cassandra craved the same thing in the boardroom that she did in the bedroom—the power to bring her adversary to their knees and have them thank her for it.

And the five men sitting across from her were about to get a taste of why she, a seemingly unassuming woman half their size, and at 35, almost half their age, was one of the most successful—and most feared—women in the corporate world.

She closed the folder of financial documents on the table before her and set it aside. "My apologies, gentlemen. There seems to be some confusion. You appear to be under the mistaken belief that this is a negotiation."

Henry blinked, his face slowly turning red. "Excuse me?"

"You heard me. You've been playing games with me for

weeks now. Stringing me along like a naive schoolgirl, something you wouldn't dare do to any of your male colleagues, might I add. I've entertained it for long enough."

She scribbled a figure on her notepad, then tore out the page and slid it across the glass conference table.

"This is my offer. My *final* offer."

Henry's eyes narrowed as he read the figure on the page. "Ms. Lee. This is…" He looked up at her. "*Cassandra—*"

She rose from her seat, her hands splayed on the table. "Take my offer. Or don't, and watch your company sink into the ground and your shareholders sue you for gross mismanagement."

Silence fell over the room. Henry looked at the men on either side of him, but all he received in return were noncommittal glances. Like Henry, they knew the reality of the situation. Harris Industries was drowning. Cassandra was the only one who could save it.

She looked at her watch. "I don't have time for this." Cassandra gathered her things from the table. "It's unfortunate that we weren't able to come to an agreement. I'm sure you'll have better luck elsewhere, gentlemen."

She took her suit jacket from the back of her chair and marched purposefully to the door, heels clicking on the marble floor of the conference room.

"Wait."

Cassandra stopped, her hand suspended above the door handle, and turned to face him. "I've done more than my fair share of waiting already."

Henry gritted his teeth. "We'll take it. We'll take the deal."

She gave him a curt nod. "I'll have the contract finalized and forwarded to you by the end of the day."

At once, the tension in the room dissipated. While Henry's irritation at being outmaneuvered was clear on his face, so was his relief. Cassandra's suspicions had been correct. He'd needed that lifeboat far more than he or his lackeys had let show. And despite Henry's objections, her offer had been fair. He could walk away with his pride intact, along with a tidy sum of money.

Cassandra stood by the door as all five men packed up their things and got up from their chairs. As each man passed her on their way out, she exchanged a handshake with them.

Henry was the last out the door. She shook his hand firmly. "It's been a pleasure."

"Wish I could say the same," he murmured.

"Let me assure you, Henry. Harris Industries is in excellent hands. I'll make sure it gets the attention it deserves. I won't let your company fail."

Henry nodded. "Thank you."

As she watched him leave, she felt a pang of satisfaction.

They always thanked her in the end.

Cassandra selected a bottle of wine from the temperature-controlled cabinet in her kitchen and popped the cork, then poured herself a generous glass before making her way to her open-plan living room. Two of the room's walls were covered in floor-to-ceiling windows, providing a breathtaking view of the night sky and the sparkling lights of the city beyond.

She sat down on her couch, sipping her wine as she took

in the cityscape. The view was one of the reasons she'd bought the penthouse apartment. It was a reminder of how far she'd come, how high she'd climbed.

She had it all. Success. Money. Power. But it wasn't greed or ambition that drove her. She didn't care about money. She didn't care about prestige. All the articles written about her career, all the magazine covers bearing her face—none of it mattered.

So why had she worked so hard all these years, clawing her way up from the bottom? It was because she knew what it was like to have nothing, no one. She knew what it was like to be desperate enough to do whatever it took to survive. She knew what it was like to be powerless.

Never again. Never again.

She released her hair from the neat bun at the base of her neck, letting her long black curls settle on her shoulders as she relaxed into her couch. That was all in the past. Her present, and her future, were hers for the taking.

That was worth celebrating, as was the deal she'd made today. It was the biggest deal of her already illustrious career. And while the vintage Bordeaux she'd opened in honor of the occasion made an excellent nightcap, she wanted something more.

She took her phone from the table, opened up her browser, and typed in the address of a website that couldn't be found on any search engine. She was looking to scratch that itch she'd had since the Harris Industries meeting, and she was willing to pay good money to do it. Because paying meant she got exactly what she needed, without the expectation of anything more.

And this particular website provided that. The exclusive escort site was aimed at a discerning clientele. Clients and escorts alike were screened and carefully curated, and the prices alone were enough to limit the clientele to the wealthy.

But that wasn't what made the site exceptional. The exclusive website specialized in clients who had unusual tastes. The kind of tastes that went far beyond sex.

Cassandra logged in and began browsing through the profiles. Among them were one or two women she'd hired before. But none of them had been able to offer her what she truly desired.

Complete and unwavering submission, body, mind, and soul. That was what Cassandra craved from a lover. Very few women had ever been able to offer her more than just a shadow of that. Some pretended well, but Cassandra could always see through their acts.

And the few who had been genuine? They'd wanted more from her. An emotional connection. A commitment. A Mistress who owned not just their body, but their heart.

And that was something Cassandra could never give them. So she'd had to cut them loose.

She continued to scroll through the profiles. Ivy. Anastasia. Cherry. All pseudonyms, of course. And all their descriptions were equally fictitious. They promised to fulfill her every fantasy, to be her perfect submissive.

But Cassandra didn't want *perfect*. She wanted *real*.

Did eschewing connections of the heart make that impossible? Could she ever find what she wanted without giving a piece of herself to another?

Never again. That was the promise she'd made to herself. She would never allow anyone else to have power over her. Her heart would never belong to anyone.

As she set down her phone, a profile at the bottom of the screen caught her eye.

Jasmine. 21. Submissive. And a photo of a young woman with red hair and hazel eyes, a scattering of freckles across her pale skin.

But it wasn't the photo that caught Cassandra's eye. It was what was written underneath it.

Virgin. Name your price. Highest bidder wins.

She was auctioning her virginity?

Cassandra picked up her phone and opened the woman's profile. There were several more photos of 'Jasmine,' which obviously wasn't her real name, along with a biography describing her as a waitress who had moved to the city a year ago. Her aspirations of going to college had led her to create the auction. The story couldn't possibly have been more cliche. Was any of it true?

It didn't matter. Cassandra had no interest in buying someone's virginity. What was virginity but a social construct that was imaginary at best, problematic at worst? And she certainly had no interest in an inexperienced lover. Not even an enticingly pretty woman with eyes that seemed to tempt Cassandra even through a screen.

But there was something about her that had Cassandra curious.

She scrolled through the woman's page. Embedded in it was a countdown timer, ending in less than ten minutes. Beneath the timer was a figure, the current highest bid.

It was almost one million dollars.

One million dollars? Who would pay so much money for something like that? But Cassandra knew exactly who. She knew the kind of person who would buy someone's virginity for a seven-figure sum. Rich. Entitled. Predatory. The kind of men she sat across the conference room table from, day after day, who had so much money and power that they felt it gave them the right to anything and anyone.

Oh, Cassandra was familiar with those people, and not only from the corporate world. She'd seen it from the other side, too. She'd seen the kind of exploitation and coercion that young women could fall prey to if they weren't careful.

Of course, Cassandra had no reason to believe this woman was being coerced or exploited. And considering her own encounters with escorts, she'd be a hypocrite if she had a problem with anyone selling their body. As long as they were doing so of their own volition, it didn't matter to her.

And yet, Cassandra felt a sense of protectiveness toward this woman. Was it because she knew what it was like to be young and desperate? Was it because she saw something of herself in the woman's face?

Was it because she found her undeniably alluring?

She examined the countdown timer again. Five minutes.

And the winning bid had gone up to 1.2 million.

She brought her wine glass to her lips and took a sip. She had no interest in this auction, or this woman. And the fact that Jasmine would probably end up sold to some rich man who got off on the idea of 'deflowering' an innocent, submissive young woman was *not* Cassandra's problem.

The numbers flickered on the screen. A new bid. 1.3

million. The numbers changed again. 1.4 million. Then 1.5 million.

Cassandra sipped her wine again. Three minutes left now. The spike in bids stopped. Who was behind them? 1.5 million dollars was an obscene amount of money, even for the wealthy.

Two minutes. One minute. A new bid for 1.8 million. On the screen, the big red bid button stared back at her, along with the woman's tempting, teasing eyes...

Cassandra shook her head. *She doesn't need you to save her.*

But there were only 30 seconds left now. And the clock was ticking.

Was she actually considering this? She closed her eyes and drew in a breath, attempting to push the idea aside. But in her mind's eye, all she could see was herself all those years ago, desperate and alone. And she could feel the helplessness of being at the mercy of another, and the *fear* that came with it, its paralyzing tendrils creeping through her body...

Cassandra steeled herself. *Never again.*

She looked at her phone. Twenty seconds left. Her thumb hovered above the screen. This was irrational. Crazy, even...

Fifteen seconds. She took a generous swig of wine, then typed in a number.

10, 9, 8...

She pressed the bid button. A loading wheel appeared in its place.

6, 5, 4...

A new bid appeared, for two million dollars.

3, 2, 1...

The countdown timer disappeared. All that remained was the winning bid.

Two million dollars. *Her* bid.

The auction was over. Cassandra had won.

'Jasmine' was hers.

CHAPTER 2

Mia stepped out of the cab, almost tripping over a crack on the sidewalk in her brand-new heels. She didn't wear heels often. Sneakers and flats were more her speed.

But tonight, she wasn't Mia. Tonight, she was *Jasmine*. And Jasmine wore high heels, red lipstick, and a little black dress. Because whoever it was that had won her auction wasn't interested in an awkward girl in jeans and a ponytail.

Well, he probably wasn't. Mia knew nothing about him. All she had was the name *Lee*. And that could be a first name or a last name.

But she did know the guy was rich. Firstly, because he'd bid two million dollars on her. Secondly, because he'd asked to meet her at The Lounge, an exclusive club downtown that was almost impossible to get into. But he'd told her in a message that he'd put her on the list. All she had to do was give her name at the door.

Still, she was a mess of nerves as she walked up the red

carpet leading to the club's entrance. It was guarded by a large man dressed in black, his tree trunk arms crossed over his wide chest.

"Uh, I'm Jasmine," she said. "Someone is waiting for me inside. Lee. I'm meeting Lee."

Without saying a word to her, the man tapped the earpiece in his ear, mumbling something under his breath. Mia shifted from one foot to the other, seconds passing in silence. What if she couldn't get in?

Finally, the man gave her a nod, stepping aside and opening the door for her. Letting out a breath of relief, she strode through it.

Inside, she was greeted by a small foyer where a woman stood waiting. She gave Mia a polite smile before taking her coat and gesturing toward the doors leading into the club itself.

"Welcome to The Lounge," she said.

Mia stepped into the room. The Lounge was nothing like the one or two clubs she'd been to before, where people were packed in like sardines, the music too loud to speak over. It was somewhere between a bar and a club, and a sophisticated one at that. The bottles of champagne being ferried around by servers and the liquor behind the bar all had labels Mia had never seen before, which had to mean they were expensive. And everyone was dressed in crisp suits, sparkling cocktail dresses and stilettos, their expensive jewelry and designer watches glittering in the soft lights of the club.

Mia smoothed down her dress. She'd bought it specifically for tonight, spending half a paycheck on it, but she didn't look anywhere near as glamorous as everyone around her. She looked just as out of place as she felt.

But it was too late to back out now.

Time to find Lee. She took her phone from her purse and sent him a message to let him know she was here, just like he'd instructed.

His reply came through almost instantly. *Come to the booth in the back left corner.*

Mia glanced toward the back of the club. Was she really doing this? Losing her virginity to a complete stranger, one who was paying her *two million dollars* for the privilege?

It was a sum of money she could hardly even comprehend. When she decided to hold the auction, she hadn't known what to expect. She'd been recommended the exclusive website by an old friend who'd signed up to make money on the side while she went to college. It was invite-only, and Mia had needed to go through a lengthy approval process which was made more complicated by the fact that she wasn't looking to offer the usual escort services. It wasn't every day that a woman wanted to sell her virginity, even on a website like that.

She'd had no idea her auction would fetch such a high price. And now it was time to deliver.

Would it happen tonight, or would they wait? Mia wasn't sure which she'd prefer. She wasn't nervous about the idea of having sex for the first time. The only reason she hadn't had sex before was because she'd never had the time for flings or relationships. She'd always had too many responsibilities. When it came to sex, she didn't have any hangups.

Sex with a stranger, though? She couldn't deny that the idea made her nervous.

But the sooner she got the money, the better. She had debts to pay, both of her own and for her family. And she'd have plenty of money left over. Enough to change her life. And her little sister's. And her mom's.

They were who she was doing this for. Her family.

Mia took a deep breath and made her way through the crowd, the pounding of her pulse audible over the beat of the music. She reached the back of the club, which was quieter, less crowded, and headed for the booth to the left.

But when Mia reached it, she found a woman sitting inside, a martini glass on the table in front of her. She wore a fitted dress made of white lace that contrasted with her wavy, jet-black hair, and a pair of black stilettos that dwarfed Mia's heels. Her lips were a deep, rich red, her eyes dark as smoke.

And those eyes were looking straight at her.

The woman rose from her seat. "Hello."

"I, uh…" Mia stumbled over her words. There was something in the woman's velvet-smooth voice that sent heat trickling through her body. "I'm sorry, I must be in the wrong place."

"You're in the right place, Jasmine."

Huh? How does she know that name?

"It *is* Jasmine, isn't it?" the woman asked. "Unless you want to tell me your real name. But I understand if you'd prefer to stick to a pseudonym for privacy."

Realization hit Mia like a bucket of cold water. "*You're Lee?*"

"Cassandra. Lee is my surname. It's Korean."

"But I thought…" Mia clamped her mouth shut. She couldn't say, *I thought you were a man*. Now that she thought about it, 'Lee' had never said as much. Mia had only assumed.

Cassandra gestured toward the seat across from her own. "Sit."

Mia took a seat. What else could she do with Cassandra looking at her the way she was? It was with a mixture of curiosity and stone-faced intensity that made Mia's heart race and her skin sizzle.

"I'm sorry." She shook her head. "I'm just a little flustered."

Cassandra sat back down. "You weren't expecting me to be a woman, were you?"

Mia shook her head again.

"I didn't intend to deceive you. I simply didn't want to give my full name until we met face to face. I have privacy concerns of my own. While I have no reservations about seeing escorts, my high profile means that if that fact became public knowledge, there would be fallout. And I do *not* have the time to deal with that."

A server stopped by their table and offered to take Mia's drink order. She simply asked for what Cassandra was having so she wouldn't have to think. It turned out to be a vodka martini.

As the server disappeared, Cassandra continued. "Is my being a woman going to be a problem?"

Mia hesitated. She didn't have any experience with women, but she didn't have much experience with anyone at all. She'd spent her whole life focused on her family. And suddenly she found herself at age 21 with zero experience beyond her overzealous imagination and a few awkward make-out sessions.

Those had been with boys, not girls. Definitely not *women*. And Cassandra was most definitely a woman. Her fitted lace dress seemed designed to enhance every element of her femininity, from the way the pale lace contrasted the warm tones of her skin and her long, dark hair, to the way the dress clung to her every captivating curve…

Mia cleared her throat. Cassandra was still waiting for an answer. "No. That's not a problem. I'm up for anything."

"So your profile said." Cassandra crossed her legs and leaned back, examining Mia with probing eyes. "It told me a lot about you. You're either desperate, naive, or both."

Mia blinked. "What?"

"You say you're a submissive," Cassandra said.

"I… yes." Mia wasn't sure if it was a statement or a question.

"What are your limits?"

Where was Cassandra going with this? "I don't have any."

"Yes, you do. Everyone does. And the fact that you think you don't only confirms what I thought." Cassandra took a sip of her drink. "Desperate. Naive. *Both*."

Mia opened her mouth to speak, but nothing came out. Why was Cassandra suddenly being so hostile?

"Why did you decide to auction off your virginity?" she asked.

Mia folded her arms across her chest. "Like my profile said, I want the money to pay for college."

"Is that all?"

"Yes." That was a lie. Other than her age, everything on her profile had been made up. She wasn't a waitress, and she'd been born right here in the city. And while she did want to go to college someday, that wasn't why she'd auctioned herself off.

The truth was much more complicated, but she hadn't wanted whoever won the auction to know just how much she needed the money. A white lie or two seemed like the safer bet.

But it was obvious from Cassandra's expression that she didn't believe Mia at all.

"So you're doing this just for the money, then?" she asked. "That's why you said you're a submissive? You thought it would help you attract a higher price?"

"What?" Mia shook her head. "No, I really am."

"How do you know that? You're clearly inexperienced. So how do you know?"

"I... I just do."

Mia glanced down at her lap, trying to hide her flushed cheeks. This wasn't going at all how she'd imagined. She hadn't expected to be interrogated.

But she wasn't lying. Not about this.

Sure, she was inexperienced. But she knew what she was. She'd known it as soon as she learned there was a word for it. It was all she'd ever desired. All she ever dreamed of.

And when she closed her eyes and her fantasies came to life, it was all she could see.

Clenching her fists in her lap, she looked up at Cassandra, their eyes locking. "I *know* I'm a submissive. I know because when I close my eyes and think about my perfect lover, they don't have a face or a form. I don't see a man, or a woman, or anything else. All I see is someone I serve with all my being, someone I belong to. Master, Mistress, it doesn't matter. What matters is I'm *theirs*."

Silence fell over them. As she gazed back at Cassandra, the rest of the club crumbled away, leaving only the two of them. And for a brief moment, she saw something in Cassandra's eyes, a glimmer, a flash of barely contained desire.

When Cassandra finally spoke, it was with a voice so low and hypnotic that it was like she was speaking directly into Mia's mind.

"Fantasy and reality are very different things, Jasmine."

"I know," Mia said. "And I know you think I'm naive, but I'm not. I didn't make this decision lightly. I'll hold up my end of the deal, as long as you do."

"Oh, I fully intend to hold up my end of the deal. But here's the thing. You were very clear about what you're offering. Anything goes. And as per the terms of your auction, it's my choice what I do with you, as long as I have your consent. I was never bidding on your virginity. I was bidding on *you*."

"W-what are you saying?"

Cassandra uncrossed her legs and leaned forward. "I don't want your virginity. I don't even want sex. What I *want* is your submission."

Mia's heart began to pound. "I don't understand."

"But you do. You're a submissive. So you know that submission isn't about sex. It's about complete and unwavering surrender. That's what I want from you. Nothing more, nothing less."

Desire flared deep in Mia's body. And in her mind, her imaginary lover coalesced. Her Master. Her Mistress.

But instead of being formless, faceless, it was *Cassandra*.

"Here's my proposal," she said. "For one month, you will be mine. My servant. My submissive. 24 hours a day, 7 days a week. Only once I'm satisfied that you truly want it will I take what's mine. And you will give it to me, freely. Not for the money, not out of obligation, but because you desire it. And if you've been telling the truth? If you're really a submissive?"

Both the woman sitting before her and the woman in Mia's head spoke in unison.

"Before the month ends, you'll be begging me to take you."

Mia's lips parted slightly, a soft breath escaping them. Cassandra had a spark in her eyes that set Mia's whole body ablaze. And for a moment, she found herself wanting Cassandra to take her there and then.

"So?" Cassandra said. "What do you say?"

Mia bit her lip. How could she agree to that? To leaving her job behind? To leaving her mom and sister behind? To leaving behind everything she'd ever known?

But under Cassandra's gaze, all those doubts, those responsibilities, didn't seem to matter. Neither did her debts, or the two million dollars that were at stake.

All that mattered was the woman sitting across from her and the sweet surrender she offered.

"I'll do it," Mia said softly.

"Then we have a deal." Cassandra sat back in her chair, her eyes never leaving Mia's. "Two million dollars is yours at the end of the month. But believe me when I say that I intend to get my money's worth, one way or another."

Heat rose to Mia's skin. For a woman who said she didn't want sex, the way Cassandra looked at her said otherwise.

"Sunday marks the start of the month. You'll move into my apartment then. I'll set up a room for you, but you'll have free use of the entire penthouse. I'm sure you'll find your accommodations pleasing."

She wants me to move in with her? Of course she did. But only now was it dawning on her what she'd agreed to. Living with a mysterious stranger in her penthouse apartment, all while being her full-time submissive, catering to her every need and whim?

What had Mia gotten herself into?

Before she could say a word, the server returned with her drink. She picked it up, gulping half of it down. It did little to settle the churning in her stomach.

"Any questions?" Cassandra asked.

Mia shook her head. But Cassandra seemed to sense her nerves.

"If you're worried about whether you can trust me to pay you, I'll have a contract drawn up outlining the terms of our agreement. But rest assured, I'm a woman of my word. Hold up your end of the deal, and I'll hold up mine."

Mia nodded mutely.

"One more thing," Cassandra said. "What's your name? Your *real* name?"

Mia swallowed another sip of her drink before setting her glass down. "It's Mia. Mia Brooks."

"Mia." The way her name rolled off Cassandra's tongue,

as if she were savoring it like a fine wine, sent a shiver rippling through her body. "You know what your name means, don't you?"

Mia nodded.

And for the first time that night, Cassandra's lips curled up in a seductive smile.

"*Mine.*"

CHAPTER 3

"Mom?" Mia called. "I'm leaving soon."

"Okay, honey!" Her mom poked her head out from the kitchen. "I'll be right there."

Mia dragged her suitcase to the door, which was no easy feat when one of its wheels was broken. As she set it down next to her bulging duffel bag, her mom emerged from the kitchen, drying her hands off with a dish towel. She'd finished a night shift at the nursing home only a couple of hours ago, and while her face was lined with fatigue, she didn't let it show in her voice.

"All ready to go?" she asked.

Mia nodded. "Just waiting for my ride. My, uh, boss is sending a car."

Her mom frowned. "I don't know about this job, Mia. Some rich woman wants you to be her live-in maid?"

That was the cover story she'd told her family. It was close enough to the truth. In a way, she *was* going to be serving Cassandra.

"I got lucky," Mia said. "Don't worry, it's totally above board, I swear."

Her mom gave a disapproving huff. "I still don't like this. You already had a perfectly good job."

"A good job? I was working at a supermarket for minimum wage. And I've been doing the same job since high school."

"Exactly. What do you know about being a maid? Why would this woman want you working for her?"

"Does it matter? The pay makes it more than worth it." She hadn't told her mom exactly how much Cassandra was paying her, just that it was a lot. "It'll be enough to pay off all of our debts. Including Holly's medical bills."

Her mom put her hands on her hips. "How many times do I have to tell you? None of that is your concern."

"Of course it is. Do you think I can just ignore the fact that we're broke? That you're killing yourself working overtime just so we can afford food? And all those overdue bills—the electric bills, the credit cards. Who do you think has been paying enough of them to keep the debt collectors off our backs?"

"And I told you, you don't need to do that."

"If I didn't, we wouldn't be able to keep the lights on!"

"If it comes to that, I can sell the house. Get something smaller."

Mia gestured around them. "This is hardly worth anything. And it's the only home Holly has ever known. The only thing we have left of Dad. We can't lose the house."

"And we won't. Not unless things get really bad. But we're not there yet. We're doing fine, I promise. You don't need to worry about money at all."

If only that were true. What her mom didn't know was that Mia had debts of her own. And the people Mia had borrowed the money from? They didn't care whether she could pay. They didn't care about the law. But she hadn't known that at the time. And she'd had no idea just how far they'd go to collect what she owed.

Not until the threats started.

She took a deep breath. *The end of the month. I'll get my money and pay off everything.*

"Honey?" her mom said. "Are you okay?"

Mia snapped herself out of her thoughts. "Yeah, I'm fine."

Before her mom could question her further, she heard the rumble of an engine outside. She looked out the front window to see a large black luxury car pulling up in front of the house.

"Looks like my ride's here," Mia said.

Her mom nodded. "Let me help you with your bag."

She opened the door and rolled Mia's suitcase outside. Mia followed, her purse and duffel bag over her shoulders. As they walked down to the car, the driver stepped out of it, greeting them politely before taking Mia's bags from her.

Her mother eyed the luxury car, one eyebrow raised. "You weren't kidding about your boss being rich. Holly is going to be mad she missed this."

"Where is Holly anyway?" Mia asked.

"Still asleep. You know how teenagers are."

It was hard to think of Holly as just another teenager. Most teenagers hadn't spent half their life in a hospital, let alone had a heart transplant.

As the driver stowed her bags in the trunk, Mia gave her

mom a warm hug. "Say goodbye to Holly for me. And tell her I love her."

"I will. And remember, you can come home whenever you want. And call me any time."

Mia broke away and hurried over to the car, where the driver stood by, holding the door open for her. With a final wave to her mom, she slipped into the back seat, thanking the driver as he shut the door.

The car pulled away from the curb. Mia watched her mother on the sidewalk through the back window, guilt rising in her stomach. She wasn't moving very far, and she'd only be gone for a month.

However, leaving her family behind still felt wrong. A lifetime of acting as a second parent to her younger sister while their mom worked to keep them afloat had left Mia with a sense of responsibility toward her.

But Holly was old enough to take care of herself now. And after the heart transplant, she'd been given as clean a bill of health as she was ever going to get. Sure, she was still on a cocktail of medications and had to see several different doctors on a regular basis. And no one knew how long it would be before she needed another heart. But for now, she was healthy, strong. She didn't need anyone to look after her. She didn't need Mia, and neither did their mom.

For the first time in her life, Mia was free to do what *she* wanted, free to experience all the things she'd missed out on because she'd had too many responsibilities. The possibilities were endless.

Well, they would be. Once she paid off her debts.

Mia lugged her bags out of the elevator. The doorman had tried to summon a bellhop to bring them up to the penthouse for her, but she'd waved him off. She had a perfectly good set of arms and legs of her own.

What kind of apartment complex has a bellhop? The kind that looked like a palace, at least on the inside. The lobby downstairs was lit by crystal chandeliers, and every surface, from the floors to the counters, was made of white marble. Even the private express elevator she'd taken up to the penthouse had polished golden walls.

Bags in tow, Mia walked down the short hallway from the elevator to the front door of the penthouse.

Taking in a deep breath, she knocked.

From the other side of the door, she heard the click of heeled footsteps getting louder. A moment later, the door opened and Cassandra appeared. Her long, dark hair was pulled back in a bun, her lips tinted a subtle scarlet. She wore a sleeveless dress in a rich, deep blue, a thin gold necklace around her neck.

The outfit was simple, plain almost. On anyone else, it wouldn't have drawn a second glance. On Cassandra?

Wow.

The first time they met, they'd been in a dark club and Mia had been so off balance that she'd barely had a chance to look at Cassandra properly. But in the light of day? Mia couldn't deny it.

Cassandra was mesmerizing.

"Good morning, Mia." She gestured inside. "Come in."

Mia stepped through the door, pulling her bags along with her, and stared around the room. The penthouse was just as lavish as the lobby, but it was much less sterile. In place of marble floors were polished floorboards and lush rugs, the furniture all made of rich leather and dark wood.

But there was nothing dark about the vast, open-plan living space. The morning sunlight shone through the floor-to-ceiling windows, which provided a stunning view of the city.

This is where I'm staying for the next month?

Cassandra broke her out of her trance. "Welcome to my home. I trust the drive here went well."

Mia nodded. "Thanks for sending the car."

"I simply want to ensure that you're comfortable during your stay here. If there's anything you need, just let me know."

"Honestly, I'm pretty easygoing. I'm sure I'll be fine."

Cassandra gave her a disapproving look. "You're going to be living here for an entire month, Mia. Don't be afraid to ask for what you need."

Mia's cheeks grew warm. "Okay."

"Now, while I'd like to give you the full tour, I need to head into work for a few hours, so I'm afraid you'll have to show yourself around."

"No problem." What kind of job did Cassandra have that she needed to work on a Sunday? Didn't being this rich mean that she could do whatever she wanted?

"You'll find everything you need in your room and in the living areas. Feel free to look around, but I'm trusting you not to look through my bedroom and my personal belongings."

"Of course." Had a part of her already considered looking through Cassandra's apartment to try to find out more about her? Maybe. But that was only because she hardly knew anything about Cassandra. Mia had searched her name online, but all she found were professional profiles and articles about her career, her achievements. None of them mentioned anything about her background or her personal life. Cassandra Lee was a complete mystery.

And the firm stare the woman was giving her was enough to quash any ideas about snooping through her apartment.

"I'll show you to your bedroom," Cassandra said. "This way."

Mia followed her deeper into the apartment, peeking into rooms as they walked. She spied a bathroom, a small guest bedroom, and a study among them.

"Here." Cassandra stopped in front of a door and opened it up. "This is it."

Mia peered into the room, then back at her. "This is *mine?*"

"For the next month? Yes."

Mia stepped inside, staring around the room in awe. It was *huge*. It had its own ensuite bathroom and a walk-in closet that was as big as her bedroom at home. And the bedroom was just as luxurious as the rest of the house. A plush leather loveseat sat by the window, and the king-sized bed was piled with a selection of pillows. She was dying to throw herself onto it, to slip underneath the cushiony covers just to find out if they were as soft as they looked.

But that would have to wait until Cassandra was gone.

Mia turned back to her. "This is perfect. Thank you."

"We're not done yet. There's more."

She led Mia into the walk-in closet. Inside, a handful of garments hung on the rails, and two pairs of brand-new heels, one in black and one in nude, were lined up on the carpeted floor beneath them.

"These are for you," Cassandra said. "I only had time to pick out a few bits and pieces, but they'll do for now."

"These are for me?" Mia glanced between Cassandra and the clothes hanging nearby. Most were covered by black garment bags, but even the bags themselves looked like they cost more than anything in Mia's wardrobe. "This is too much. I can't accept this. I have plenty of clothes of my own to wear."

"I'm sure you do. But if you're going to be mine for a month, you need to look the part." Cassandra plucked a garment bag from the rail and hung it on a hook by the door. "We're having dinner tonight to discuss our arrangement in more detail. Wear this dress."

Mia eyed the garment bag warily. Cassandra was choosing outfits for her, dressing her up like a doll? Was this what it meant to be her live-in submissive? To have every element of her life controlled by Cassandra?

Why did the idea send a thrill through Mia?

"Is that going to be a problem?" Cassandra asked.

Mia shook her head. "No."

"Good. And wear your hair up tonight. It will go better with the dress." Cassandra looked at her watch. "I need to get going. Come."

She ushered Mia out of the room. Mia followed her to the table by the door, where Cassandra produced a set of keys. She handed them to Mia, explaining that one opened the front door, and the other allowed her to access the express elevator up to the penthouse.

"And if you need anything while I'm gone, call the building's concierge and he'll arrange it," she said. "The number is by the phone. I'm trusting that you won't abuse the privileges I'm giving you. I do not appreciate being taken advantage of. Break my trust and there *will* be consequences."

Mia nodded. It was only natural that Cassandra was wary. After all, she'd invited a complete stranger into her home. Until now, it hadn't occurred to Mia that it wasn't just *her* who was risking it all in their agreement.

"I believe that's everything." Cassandra slipped on a pair of glossy black heels and grabbed her coat from the stand by the door. "You have my number if you need it. Otherwise, make yourself at home. I'll be back this afternoon."

She opened the front door. But before she stepped through it, she turned and looked over her shoulder. "And Mia?"

"Yes?"

"Be a good girl while I'm gone."

Warmth rose to Mia's skin. Her lips parted soundlessly, her mouth suddenly too dry to form words. Why did she feel so hot and flushed? What was this fluttery, tingly feeling?

She pulled herself together. But Cassandra had already stepped outside. And the last thing Mia saw as the door closed was a hint of a smile on Cassandra's lips.

Good girl.

They were just words. Two little words.

So why had they turned Mia into a helpless puddle of desire?

CHAPTER 4

Cassandra stepped out of the elevator onto the top floor of her office building. During the week, the offices were packed with people, but on weekends, they were entirely deserted. She made a point of not allowing her employees to work weekends except in exceptional circumstances. While Cassandra respected hard work, she also saw the value of not working her employees to death.

Was it hypocritical, then, that she often worked weekends herself? Perhaps. But as CEO and owner of the company, overtime was a necessity for her.

Or so she told herself as she made her way to her office. But she only planned to stay for a couple of hours to get a few time-sensitive tasks done. The Harris acquisition meant her workload had increased drastically. Which made her decision to take Mia on as a live-in submissive even more illogical.

She reached her office, a large corner room with a view that rivaled that of her penthouse, and shut the door behind her. Setting down the newspaper and coffee she'd picked up downstairs, she took a seat behind her desk.

As she settled into her leather chair, she opened up the newspaper, skimming the headlines. Like everyone else, she got most of her news online. But this, along with the double espresso she drank, was a ritual of sorts, one she performed every morning.

This morning, however, she barely took in a word she read. Her mind was still on Mia.

That wasn't surprising. After all, she'd made Mia her live-in submissive on a whim. When she went to The Lounge to meet her that night, she hadn't intended to propose such an agreement. It had been a compromise, a solution to a problem. Because she'd had no intention of having a one-night stand with Mia either.

And meeting her in person had only confirmed everything Cassandra already thought about her. With teasing curves, hazel eyes that sparkled blue and green, and hair a playful shade of red, the hunger she stirred within Cassandra was impossible to ignore. But in her little black dress and heels, Mia had been playing dress-up. She was out of her depth. Too naive. Too innocent.

Too much like Cassandra had once been.

And just like her, Mia was innately drawn to the kinky side of life. Cassandra had seen it in her eyes. She'd heard it in her voice when she spoke of the images she saw when she closed her eyes. *All I see is someone I serve with all my being, someone I belong to. Master, Mistress, it doesn't matter. What matters is I'm theirs.*

But the intensity of her words, the yearning in them—it was dangerous. If Mia trusted the wrong person with those desires, she'd only end up hurt. She needed someone to guide her, someone who could help her explore them safely.

And Cassandra could be that someone.

For 30 days, Mia would be hers. And for 30 days, she would give Cassandra her unwavering submission.

If anything more happened between them? So be it. But submission wasn't about sex. Any experienced Domme knew that.

She flipped through the newspaper. Was it dangerous, taking on someone as inexperienced as Mia? Someone who didn't know her limits, who hadn't experienced the heights and depths of emotion that total surrender could bring? It was so easy to get caught up in those feelings. Easy to mistake them for something more.

But this arrangement of theirs had a time limit. And one month wasn't long enough for a true connection to form between them, for lines to blur. Still, Cassandra had to take care not to give Mia the wrong impression. Because Cassandra's heart was her own.

She folded up the newspaper. As she set it aside, she caught a glimpse of a headline at the bottom of the front page that she'd somehow missed.

Diane Whiteford Secures Early Release From Prison

Cassandra closed her eyes and leaned back in her chair. *So this is it.* She'd been keeping tabs on the story for months and she'd always known this day was coming. But she'd kept it locked up in the back of her mind, unable, *unwilling*, to face it.

Now, there was no ignoring it. Her past had finally caught up with her.

She picked up her personal phone, dialing a number she

had on speed-dial. It only took a few rings for the person at the other end to answer.

"Riley," she said. "I need to speak to you immediately."

∼

"Thank you for coming by." Cassandra shut her office door and returned to sit behind her desk. "I know it's unusual for me to meet you at the office, but this is a matter of urgency."

Riley sat down in a chair opposite Cassandra and crossed their legs. They were dressed in a navy-blue blazer and pants with a t-shirt underneath, which was their idea of casual clothing.

"What do you need from me?" they asked.

"Security," Cassandra replied. "I need security for my office and my apartment. All discreet, of course."

"Sure. Let me give you some names, put you in touch with some people."

"No. I want you to oversee this personally. Hire whoever you need."

"Okay. But…" Riley ran their fingers through their short, dark hair. "You could hire an entire specialist security firm for what this is going to cost you. You know that, right?"

"I do."

"And you know I prefer to work alone. I don't play well with others."

"I'm aware. But I'm asking you to make an exception. I need someone I can trust. This is a sensitive matter."

Riley waited for her to say more. When she didn't, they sat forward, clasping their hands together with their elbows perched on their knees. "Is there a threat to your person? Do you need personal security, too?"

"That won't be necessary. Not for now, at least." Cassandra was far too high-profile for Di—for *Diane*—to dare come after her directly.

Besides, that wasn't her style.

"What about the Queens Club?" Riley asked. "Do you need a security team there?"

Cassandra shook her head. The Queens Club already had a robust security system. And the exclusive club's existence wasn't known to anyone other than its members. She didn't need security guards lurking around, drawing attention.

"Just keep an eye on the club yourself when you can," she said. "But focus on my office and my apartment. Money is not an obstacle, so spare no expense."

Riley cocked their head to the side. "Why do you need all this security in the first place?"

Cassandra slid her tablet across the table. On its screen was a headshot of a raven-haired woman. "This is Diane Whiteford. She was recently released from prison. I have reason to believe that she may try to harm me."

Riley examined the photo of Diane. She looked just like any other middle-aged, upper-class white woman. But Cassandra knew better. She knew who Diane really was.

After all, Cassandra was the one who had exposed her.

"Diane Whiteford..." Riley narrowed their eyes. "Why is that name familiar?"

Cassandra ignored the question. "Make sure everyone you hire is aware that they need to keep an eye out for this woman. I'll send you her information so you can distribute it to them. Despite appearances, she's dangerous. I *cannot* stress this enough."

"Understood." Riley handed the tablet back to Cassandra. "I have contacts at some top-notch security firms. I'll reach out to them, get them to send me a couple of teams. I'll oversee everything personally. Make sure you have the best."

Cassandra nodded. "Thank you. Let me know if there's anything you need."

Riley got to their feet. "I will."

"And remember, discretion is paramount." The last thing she needed was anyone finding out that there was a connection between her and Diane.

The last thing she needed was anyone finding out about her past.

Riley nodded. "Understood."

As they left the room, Cassandra made a mental list of all the other people she needed to contact. While she trusted Riley, she couldn't rely solely on them and whatever security they hired to keep an eye out for Diane. She needed to make use of some of her other contacts, not all of whom were above board.

But that could wait. She had plenty of work to do. It was already afternoon, and she'd barely made a dent in it. She'd need to stay at the office and go straight to the restaurant to meet Mia for dinner.

Mia. Naive, innocent, Mia. So innocent, in fact, that she'd simply melted when Cassandra spoke just a few simple words to her this morning.

She'd be lying if she said she hadn't known exactly what

she was doing. But she hadn't expected such a strong reaction from Mia.

And what she'd expected even less was just how much pleasure she'd taken in Mia's reaction.

She leaned back in her chair, a smile pulling at her lips.

Could it be that, despite Mia's inexperience, she was exactly what Cassandra was looking for?

CHAPTER 5

The maitre d' pulled a chair out from under the table and waited for Mia to take a seat. She sat down, mumbling a thank you as she looked around the small but elegant French restaurant. The table Cassandra had booked them was up on a mezzanine that overlooked the rest of the room, providing them with a little privacy.

Mia glanced at her phone. She was still a few minutes early. Cassandra hadn't come home this afternoon. Instead, she'd sent a car to pick Mia up and drive her to the restaurant, promising to meet her there.

She slipped her phone back into her purse and smoothed down the skirt of her dress. She'd worn the outfit Cassandra had picked out for her, which turned out to be a silky cocktail dress in a deep, vivid green. It was fitted at the top before flaring out at the waist, and while it wasn't short enough to scandalize, it was shorter than anything Mia would have chosen for herself.

Not that she ever chose to wear anything so fancy in the first place. When she wasn't in her work uniform, she wore t-shirts and jeans, usually paired with sneakers. She didn't have the time or energy to think about fashion.

But this dress? It was undeniably fashionable. And paired with the nude heels from the closet in her room, which were exactly the right size, it made her legs look much longer than they were. The overall look was sexy but sophisticated.

Would Cassandra think so, too?

As if on cue, Cassandra appeared at the top of the stairs, the maitre d' at her heels. She was dressed the same as in the morning, but her hair hung loose now, her dark waves framing elegant cheekbones.

The maitre d' led her to the table, but he didn't pull a chair out for her like he had for Mia. He simply waited until Cassandra was seated before informing them that a waiter would be with them shortly.

As he disappeared down the stairs, Cassandra turned to her. "You wore the dress. That's good. You know how to follow orders." Her eyes traveled up Mia's body. "That color suits you. It brings out your eyes."

Warmth crept up Mia's cheeks. "T-thank you." Why did she feel like she was sixteen and going on her first date again?

Cassandra opened up her menu. "Would you like some help with what to order?"

Mia glanced at her own menu. It took her far too long to realize that the reason she couldn't read it wasn't because she was flustered but because it was in French. "Sure. That would be great."

Cassandra described each of the dishes on the menu, offering her recommendations. There were no prices on them, which had to mean they were astronomical. But Mia wasn't the one paying.

Finally, she chose the dish that seemed the least intimidating, something with roasted chicken and a truffle sauce. A waiter came by and took their orders, followed by a sommelier. Cassandra listened to his suggestions before choosing for them both, selecting a wine for Mia that would pair well with her meal.

Once their glasses had been filled, Cassandra returned her attention to Mia. "I apologize for leaving you alone in the apartment all day. I didn't intend to spend so long in the office, but something came up."

"It's fine," Mia said quickly. "You don't have to worry about me."

"Now, there's no need to be so nervous, Mia. We're going to be living together for a month. I want you to feel comfortable with me. But that will come as we get to know each other. We're practically strangers, after all. And I'm sure you must be just as curious about me as I am about you."

"You're… curious about me?"

"Of course." Cassandra swirled her wine around in her glass before raising it to her lips, sampling it. "To start with, I've been wondering what kind of life you lead that you were able to pick up and move in with me in the space of a few days. There aren't many people who have so few obligations. You were working as a waitress, correct?"

Mia hesitated. "Actually, that was a lie, like my name. I worked at a supermarket, but I quit a few days ago. It was a terrible job, anyway."

"Oh? And what about everything else in your profile? How much of that was fiction?"

"Most of it," Mia admitted. "I do want to go to college, though."

"And that's why you auctioned yourself off?"

"Among other things. My family doesn't have a lot of money. My little sister Holly was born with a heart condition. All of her medical costs have taken a toll over the years. I want to help with that too. Pay off her medical bills and some other debts."

"I'm sorry to hear about your sister," Cassandra said. "How is she doing now?"

"She's doing great. When she was younger, she was in and out of the hospital constantly, but those days are over now. Which is a relief, because things were really hard for her growing up. And for our mom. Our dad died when I was six, just after Holly was born, so Mom was on her own. I started helping once I got older."

"That must have been hard for you, too."

Mia shrugged. "It was much harder for Holly. But like I said, things are better now." She picked up her wine glass and took a tentative sip, then another. It was *really* good wine. "What about you? Do you have any family?"

"None that matters," Cassandra said. "I haven't spoken with my family in a long time."

"Oh. I'm sorry."

"Don't be." Cassandra reached down into her large, stylish purse and pulled out a tablet. "Now, let's get down to it. I've put together a little something outlining all the details of our arrangement."

That was a quick change of subject. "You mean, the contract?" Mia asked.

"That's right. Here."

Cassandra slid the tablet across the table. On the screen was a document with both of their names at the top, followed by a bunch of legalese.

Mia took the tablet and scrolled through the pages. The first one covered everything they'd already discussed. Mia would be Cassandra's live-in submissive for 30 days, and at the end of the month she'd receive a sum of two million dollars.

But the contract wasn't only about the financial details of their arrangement. As she flicked through it, she was faced with page after page outlining exactly what Cassandra expected of her submissive, in *intimate* detail.

The submissive will obey her Dominant unless doing so will cause harm to herself or others.

The submissive will address her Dominant as "Mistress" or "Mistress Cassandra" during scenes and when otherwise instructed.

The submissive will not touch the Dominant without her permission.

The submissive will be available to her Dominant at all times—

Mia's skin began to burn. *Available?* For what, exactly? She glanced up at Cassandra, but the woman's face remained stone. Did she really expect Mia to sign away her freedom like this?

Butterflies flitted in her stomach. Why didn't the idea bother her?

Why did it excite her instead?

She read on, skimming through the endless list of requirements.

The submissive's body belongs to her Dominant... She will maintain a healthy lifestyle and take care of her physical and mental wellbeing... She will dress as instructed by her Dominant... She will not pleasure herself in any way without her Mistress's permission...

Mia read the clause again. *Seriously? I can't even... seriously?*

"Everything in the agreement beyond the basic terms is negotiable," Cassandra said. "And it isn't set in stone once we sign it. Amendments can be made. I'm sure you'll realize very quickly that you do, in fact, have limits, so we'll need to write those into the agreement. Along with a safe word. That will need to be established before we do anything."

Limits? Safe words? This was suddenly starting to feel very, very real.

"Is everything all right?" Cassandra asked.

"This is just... a lot."

"As I said, it's all negotiable. We can revisit the terms at any time. That fact is even written into the contract. That's the first thing you need to understand. An arrangement like this is built on consent and communication. I expect you to speak up about your needs."

Mia nodded. Even that was in the contract. *The submissive will communicate her needs along with any issues or concerns to her Dominant...*

"Do you have any questions?" Cassandra asked.

Mia chewed her lip in thought. "Well, I do have a few. And not just about all this. About you, too."

"Go on."

"So, this arrangement. This contract. Is it something you've done before?"

Cassandra picked up her wine glass and took a sip. "In a way. I usually prefer more casual arrangements. And normally, they're a one-off with an experienced professional. In those cases, contracts this detailed are unnecessary."

"So you've hired a submissive before?"

"How do you think I found your auction? Paying someone to give me exactly what I need is much simpler than navigating casual encounters or relationships."

"And those people. They were all women?"

Cassandra nodded. "I'm not interested in men. I never have been."

Mia studied the woman's face. Cassandra seemed entirely unfazed by her questions. Mia was just as jealous of her unshakable confidence as she was drawn to it.

Mia continued to scroll through the pages of the document. "So, this contract. It doesn't say anything about, well… sex."

"That's correct," Cassandra said. "Like I said, sex isn't a necessary part of submission."

"So, the other women you've done this with? Did you have sex with them?"

"Some of them. But first and foremost, I want a submissive, not a lover. So sex is only on the table if I'm sure that it will be satisfying for the other person, that they're someone who takes genuine pleasure from submission. People like that are rare."

That explained a lot. But there was still one question on

Mia's mind. "If you prefer experienced women, why did you bid on my auction?"

For the first time since they met, Cassandra seemed to hesitate.

"It was a whim," she finally said. "Nothing more."

A whim? Who would spend two million dollars on a whim? And to buy someone's virginity? Although, it was clear that Cassandra wasn't even interested in her virginity.

So why had she bought it?

But Cassandra didn't elaborate. "Now, if you'd like more time to look over the contract, I can send you a copy."

Mia shook her head. "I want to sign it now. Let's do it."

Cassandra took the tablet back from her and produced a stylus, scrawling her signature at the bottom of the last page before handing both to Mia, who did the same.

"Then it's settled." Cassandra set the tablet aside, her dark eyes fixed on Mia's. "For the next 30 days, you belong to me."

Her pulse began to race. Thirty days as Cassandra's servant, her submissive. Thirty days living in her apartment, catering to her every whim. And if Cassandra wanted the thing that Mia had sold to her in the first place, she would give her that too.

She was Cassandra's now. There was no turning back.

CHAPTER 6

Where's my money? It's time to pay up.

Mia's stomach tightened, the Thai takeout she was eating threatening to come back up. She set her phone aside and continued with her dinner, but she couldn't get the message off her mind.

It had come from a man she was uncomfortably familiar with. She only knew him by a single name—Bruno. And that name carried a reputation, one she couldn't ignore.

She picked up her phone again and typed out a reply.

I'll have it for you at the end of the month. Just give me until then.

She pressed send. Seconds passed, then minutes, but no response arrived. Which was worse? Silence or threats?

Mia pushed her food around on her plate. She'd only eaten half her dinner, but she'd lost her appetite.

The clink of keys in the front door of the penthouse broke through her thoughts. It was just past 8 p.m. Was Cassandra finally home from work? It had only been a couple of days since Mia moved in, but Cassandra had spent the entire time working.

Why did she want a live-in submissive when she was hardly ever home? Why did she bid on Mia in the first place? Her explanation, that it was just a whim, didn't make any sense. Two million dollars was a lot of money, even for someone like Cassandra.

As the front door opened, Mia got to her feet. Her Mistress had arrived. She was carrying not only the stylish purse that served as her briefcase but a pair of black shopping bags.

Cassandra greeted Mia, setting her bags down on the table near the door.

"I bought some takeout for dinner," Mia said. "I hope that's okay." Cassandra had given her a credit card with the caveat that she use it for food and other essentials only. She didn't specify what counted as essential, but Mia didn't dare test Cassandra's boundaries.

"It's fine," she replied. "That's what I gave you the card for."

She slipped off her coat and hung it up, revealing a sleeveless dress and toned arms underneath. Mia followed the line of her bare shoulder to her delicate collarbone, up her neck, up to her lips, red and luscious…

Cassandra's dark eyes met hers. Mia's cheeks began to burn. She hadn't meant to stare.

"There are leftovers," Mia said quickly. "They're in the fridge if you want some."

"I ate at work."

"Well, is there anything I can do for you?"

Instead of answering her, Cassandra sauntered over to

where Mia stood, hips swaying. "So eager to serve, aren't you?"

Mia's heartbeat quickened. "I just... I want to..."

Cassandra reached up and took Mia's chin in her fingers gently. "All in due time, Mia. All in due time."

She drew her hand back but Mia could still feel her touch lingering on her skin.

As Cassandra stepped into the kitchen, she sat back down, her stomach fluttering. Once again, she found she couldn't eat, but for an entirely different reason.

"Would you like a glass of wine?" Cassandra said from the kitchen.

"No, I'm fine." Mia had seen Cassandra's wine collection. Whatever she chose would be wasted on Mia, who couldn't tell the difference between a ten-dollar bottle and a one-hundred-dollar one.

"Are you sure? Why don't I bring the bottle to the table? Then you can decide."

Cassandra didn't wait for an answer before returning to the dining table, two glasses in one hand and a bottle of white wine in the other. She opened the bottle and poured herself a glass, the wine's sweet aroma filling the air.

Cassandra picked up the glass and swirled it around before taking a sip. "Magnificent." She let out a satisfied sigh. "Are you sure you don't want some? It's very good."

"Okay. Why not?" Maybe it would help settle Mia's stomach and her nerves.

Cassandra poured another glass and pushed it across the table to her. Mia sipped it slowly. Cassandra was right. It *was* good.

"Now, we need to talk about this arrangement of ours,"

she said. "The contract is signed and you're all settled in. It's time for us to get down to business."

Mia swallowed. "S-sure. Whatever you want."

"Whatever I want?" Cassandra peered at her from over the top of her wine glass. "We'll find out if you still feel the same way after Friday night."

"Friday night?"

"That's right. I have plans for us."

What kind of plans? But if Cassandra wanted her to know, she'd tell her.

Cassandra nodded toward the black shopping bags on the table by the door. "You'll need to dress appropriately, so I've picked up a little something for you to wear."

"Those are for me?" The glossy black bags had gold writing on them and looked to be from some kind of boutique.

"That's right. You may open them after you finish your dinner."

Mia picked up her fork. Why didn't it bother her that Cassandra was ordering her around like a child? She was a grown woman. And she'd been looking after her sister and herself since she was old enough. She didn't need to be told what to do, when to eat. Yet, a part of her didn't mind it.

Besides, her own feelings didn't matter. This arrangement of theirs was purely transactional, and Mia's role in the transaction was to cater to whatever Cassandra wanted. Was that any different from her usual life? She'd always put her family's needs first, even before her own.

She finished off her dinner and began clearing the table, but Cassandra interrupted her. "Leave it. Go open the gifts I bought you. But take them to your room first, okay?"

Mia nodded. "Okay."

"Good girl."

Mia scrambled to grab the bags, taking them into her bedroom and shutting the door hard behind her. Why had she run off like that? Maybe it was because she needed to collect herself after hearing the words "good girl" roll off Cassandra's velvet tongue once again.

Why did her words make Mia's pulse throb, her voice set Mia's body alight? The woman was reserved, cold, prickly even. Yet just a look from Cassandra sent heat rising through her for no real reason at all.

No, there was a reason for it. It was because Cassandra was everything Mia desired. Her beauty. Her confidence. Her graceful but dominant manner.

Mia took a few deep breaths. It was time to find out what Cassandra had gifted her.

She set the bags down on her bed and opened up the larger of the two, reaching into it and pulling out what was inside.

Another dress? There were already several in the closet, bought and paid for by Cassandra. But this one was different. It was short and slinky, with spaghetti straps and a low back, and it was made of black and silver fabric that shimmered and glittered in the light.

"Wow." Mia laid the dress out carefully on the bed. While it was just as elegant as the dress she'd worn to dinner the other night, it was far more glamorous. Far more *risque*.

But *risque* wasn't Mia's style. Would being Cassandra's submissive mean getting out of her comfort zone in every way, down to the way she dressed? She'd never dreamed of wearing something like this.

But was that just because she hadn't had the luxury of giving thought to what she wore in the first place?

Mia took the other bag and opened it up. It was smaller than the first, and half filled with tissue paper. She pulled back the paper, uncovering what was inside.

Is that... lingerie?

Mia upended the bag, spilling its contents out onto the bed. *Yup. Lingerie.* A strapless bra and a matching pair of panties, both dark as night and made of sheer, fine lace.

Mia's skin grew hot. Cassandra had bought her *lingerie*?

Did that mean she expected to see Mia wearing it?

She shook her head. She was reading too much into it. The dress's spaghetti straps meant wearing a strapless bra or nothing, so maybe Cassandra was simply providing her with something she could wear underneath. But the bra obviously wasn't designed for support. And the matching lace panties? Why would Mia need those?

She stuffed the lingerie back in the bag. One thing was becoming more and more clear. Cassandra liked to keep her guessing.

So where were they going on Friday night?

CHAPTER 7

"Welcome," Cassandra said, shaking the woman's hand. "Have a seat."

She gestured toward the chair in front of her desk. It was evening, but instead of going home after work, she'd traded one office for another, one meeting for another. Now, she sat behind her desk in her office on the top floor of the old sandstone building that served as Queens Club headquarters. And instead of a meeting with yet another identical corporate suit, she was meeting with Penelope Grant, entrepreneur and soon-to-be club member.

The auburn-haired woman took a seat. *Penelope Grant. 33 years old. From a working-class background, spent the past 5 years rising up the ranks to become one of the most successful entrepreneurs on the east coast. Has two thriving startups under her belt.*

In other words, the perfect Queens Club member. Cassandra had tried to invite Penelope to join the club more than once over the past few years, without success. She was a hard woman to pin down, and she preferred to keep to herself. Cassandra could understand that.

"I'm glad you finally decided to accept my invitation," Cassandra said. "You must be wondering what all this is about."

Penelope crossed one leg over the other. "You could say that. Your invitation was vague at best."

"There's a reason for that. But let me start from the beginning." Cassandra gestured around them. "This building serves as the headquarters of the Queens Club, an exclusive private members' club for women."

The Queens Club was Cassandra's crown jewel. She'd built it from the ground up all by herself. It meant more to her than her career, more than anything else in her life. Because unlike everything else, it was bigger than just her.

Penelope folded her arms across her chest. "I can't say I've ever heard of this club."

"That's by design. Only our members know of the Queens Club's existence. That's why I had to be so cryptic in my invitation, and why I had you sign an NDA before we even walked through the doors. The club's members include some of the most powerful and influential women on the continent. Some, like you and I, are businesswomen. Some are politicians, celebrities. Privacy is paramount."

"All right. And why should I join this club of yours?"

Cassandra folded her hands on her desk. "I understand why you'd be wary of such institutions. I am myself, which was why I started the Queens Club. While it's modeled off the gentlemen's clubs of old, its purpose is to be the antithesis of them. It's a way for women to get a leg up in the world. Especially women like us."

"Women like us?"

"Self-made women. Women who came from nothing. Women who have had to deal with sexism, nepotism, homophobia, and still managed to claw our way up the ladder."

Penelope raised an eyebrow. "You seem to know a lot about me."

"I did my research. I always do when inviting someone to join the Queens Club. And I'm sure you looked into me before coming here."

Penelope's silence was confirmation enough.

"Let me put it another way," Cassandra said. "You're a businesswoman. So I'm sure you can understand how vital connections are. That's what the Queens Club is about. Connecting with like-minded people, helping each other out."

Women like us need to stick together. That was one of the many lessons Cassandra had learned from Diane. She hated how much she owed Diane for her success.

"A compelling argument," Penelope murmured.

"There are other, more material benefits. We have a range of amenities available to members, both across the country and here at headquarters. This building serves as a valuable private space for networking and socializing. On top of the bar and dining room, we have recreational facilities including a gym, a sauna, a heated indoor lap pool. And we have overnight suites and meeting spaces, all in the heart of the city. I'm sure you saw some of these facilities on the way in, but I'm happy to give you the full tour."

"No need. I've seen enough." Penelope gave her a nod. "You've talked me into it."

"Wonderful. I'll get the paperwork together."

Cassandra brought up the relevant documents on her tablet. A membership contract. Club rules. Another, more detailed non-disclosure agreement.

Once all were signed, Penelope announced she had an engagement to go to. As Cassandra led her out the door and down the hall to the elevator, a question formed in her mind.

"What was it that made you decide to finally accept my invitation to come here?" she asked.

A slight smile crossed Penelope's lips. "When I looked into you, I learned we have quite a lot in common. Let's just say this isn't the only exclusive club we're both a part of."

The elevator arrived. With a polite farewell, Penelope disappeared inside it.

Cassandra returned to her office to pack up her desk. It was time to go home. Home, where Mia was waiting, eager to please, ready to serve. She was the perfect piece of forbidden fruit.

And how delicious it will be to make her mine.

Cassandra leaned back in her chair, closing her eyes for just a moment. *Friday night. That will be the real test. That will reveal whether Mia is truly ready to be mine.*

But Mia would never really be hers. She would never be more than a temporary plaything. Their arrangement was contractual. Cassandra couldn't forget that.

Her phone vibrated on her desk. She picked it up. There was a message, consisting of just a few words.

9 p.m. The park, near the fountain.

Cassandra slipped her phone into her bag. She had one more stop to make before she went home.

SAVING MIA

Cassandra arrived at the park with a few minutes to spare. The sun had long set, a fall breeze cooling the air, but there were still plenty of people about. Dog walkers. Joggers. Couples on late-night strolls.

And sitting on a bench by the fountain was the woman she was due to meet. She was around Cassandra's age and was dressed in yoga pants and a designer coat, two meticulously groomed poodles leashed to the bench beside her. Her hair was dyed a light brown, but her face was the same as Cassandra remembered.

Cassandra approached the bench and took a seat next to her. "Kimberly."

The woman gave her a small nod. "Hi, Cassie."

Cassandra bristled at the sound of her old nickname. It was from a past life, one she'd long left behind her.

Yet here she was.

"It's been a while," Kimberly said. "I was surprised to hear from you. Then I saw the news."

"So you've heard?"

"That Di got out early? Yeah. Can't say I'm surprised. Rich bitches like her always get off easy. Maybe if people knew about all the other stuff she did, she'd have stayed locked up for longer."

"Has she tried to get in touch with you?" All of Cassandra's other contacts had reported that they hadn't heard a thing from Diane. Kimberly was the only person Cassandra hadn't spoken to yet.

She shook her head. "I haven't heard from her. And to be honest, I doubt she even remembers me. It's been so long."

If only I was so lucky. Diane would never forget Cassandra. "Have you heard from any of the others?"

"We don't really talk anymore. We've all moved on from that life."

"I understand. I'm sorry for dragging you back into it."

"It's okay. I still owe you for helping me out."

"That was years ago. And it was nothing." Cassandra had gotten her out of some trouble as a favor. It had been a rare moment of generosity. But she had a soft spot for those who were desperate and struggling because life had been cruel to them.

Just like Mia? That was why Cassandra had bid on her, wasn't it? To save her from a fate like her own?

She pushed the thought aside. "You seem to be doing well for yourself." If the designer clothes and dogs hadn't made that much obvious, the grape-sized ring on her left ring finger did.

Kimberly smiled. "I'll say. I'm a married woman now. He used to be one of my regulars. He was really sweet and handsome, just kind of awkward with the ladies. But he treated me well and one thing led to another, and next thing you know, we're married."

"Congratulations."

"Thanks. I'm not going to lie. I was only in it for the money at first, and so my kid would have a good life, but eventually, I fell in love with him. We have another kid together now, too."

Cassandra gave her a small smile. "I'm happy for you. And I'm glad you were able to move on from everything."

"What about you?" Kimberly asked. "Sure, you're doing great. I mean, you're *Cassandra Lee*. I've seen the magazine covers. I've read the articles. But have you moved on? Like, really moved on?"

"I put that life behind me long ago."

"Then why are you trying to find out what Di is up to?"

"Because I *have* moved on. I've built a new life for myself. So I need to protect it."

"You think she's going to come after you?" Kimberly searched Cassandra's face. "It was you who turned her in, wasn't it? No, on second thought, I don't want to know. I don't want to get involved in anything to do with Diane. I'm not putting myself in her crosshairs."

"Then I won't trouble you any further." Cassandra rose to her feet. "But if she does reach out, let me know immediately."

For your sake, as well as mine. Because Diane Whiteford was dangerous. Cassandra knew that better than anyone. She didn't forget. She didn't forgive. She'd probably spent her time in prison stoking her grudge against Cassandra, plotting her revenge, her punishment.

And it was only a matter of time before she made her move.

CHAPTER 8

Mia gazed around them. "What is this place?"

Friday night had finally arrived. She'd waited for Cassandra to get home from work. She'd dressed up in the lingerie and dress Cassandra had bought her, as instructed. Then the two of them left the penthouse and got into a car, which had driven them downtown.

And now, they were inside some kind of club.

"This is Lilith's Den," Cassandra said. "It's one of the most exclusive clubs in the city. No one can set foot inside without an invitation, for obvious reasons."

No kidding. It wasn't just any club. Sure, there was a bar, and tables and chairs, and music. But in a nearby corner, a set of metal cuffs and shackles were built right into the wall. Beside them was what looked like an umbrella stand, except instead of umbrellas, it was filled with riding crops and canes. And a few feet from that was a strange bench that looked like it was meant for restraining someone. It had an array of ropes of different lengths and colors hanging on the wall above it.

And the people? While some wore designer dresses or suits, others were dressed in leather and lingerie. And one of those leather-clad women was holding a fearsome-looking whip in her hand.

No, this wasn't just any club. Lilith's Den was a BDSM club.

Mia glanced at Cassandra. How could she just stand there when there was a woman wearing nothing but a blindfold and panties being led around by the collar, right before their eyes?

"Don't worry," Cassandra said. "That's not going to be you tonight. That's not what we're here for. Besides…" She leaned in close, speaking into Mia's ear. "If I wanted to strip you down to your panties, I'd do it in private. Tonight, it's just enough to know you're wearing what I bought you."

Heat crept up Mia's cheeks. Was that the reason Cassandra had told her to wear the lingerie? Because it satisfied her to know that Mia was wearing it?

"Come," Cassandra said. "Let's get a drink."

She placed her hand on the back of Mia's arm, leading her deeper into the club. Mia's skin tingled, the heat on her face spreading through her whole body.

What was it about Cassandra that left her so hot and bothered? Was it the way she carried herself, so confident and commanding that she turned heads even in a place like this? Or was it the effortless way she balanced sexiness with elegance? In her fitted black off-the-shoulder dress, her hair pulled up to reveal her bare neck and shoulders, and heels that drew attention to her endless legs, Mia couldn't stop staring at her.

Cassandra led her to the bar, where they each ordered a

drink. Mia tried not to gawk at the people around her while she waited. But that was easier said than done. While some of the crowd were behaving just like they would at a nightclub, drinking and dancing and flirting, others were engaged in far more explicit activities. And they weren't shy about it either.

Cassandra handed Mia her drink, studying her with probing eyes. "What's going through your mind right now?"

"I don't know what to think," Mia said. "I've never seen anything like this before."

"Does it make you uncomfortable, being among all this?"

Mia shook her head. "It's actually kind of... exciting."

"Oh?" Cassandra raised her martini glass to her ruby-red lips, sipping slowly. "And what about this excites you?"

"I don't know. It's nothing in particular. It's just a feeling. It's hard to put it into words."

Mia looked around the room, her eyes landing on a pair of women sitting nearby. One sat on an armchair with a stiff, high back, almost like a throne. The other knelt on the floor at her feet, her hands bound together with leather cuffs. Attached to the cuffs was a leash, the other end held by the woman on the throne.

She reached down, caressing the face of the woman on the floor. The woman gazed up at her Mistress, her eyes shimmering with adoration.

"It's... it's that," Mia said. "That's what excites me. That feeling, that idea of surrendering to another so completely. When I look at her, I want to know what that feels like. I want to feel what she feels."

She glanced at Cassandra, her stomach fluttering. Cassandra was looking back at her, silently searching her face. And in her eyes was a kind of curiosity, mixed with an unmistakable lust.

"There's something I want to show you," she said. "Finish your drink, but don't rush."

Mia obeyed, finishing off her drink as quickly as she could without gulping the whole thing down. Cassandra took her empty glass from her and placed it back on the bar alongside her own, then placed her hand on the small of Mia's back, sending electricity sparking through her.

"Come," she said.

Mia's pulse raced. Was there a possessiveness in the way Cassandra touched her? She'd already marked Mia by dressing her up in the expensive clothes she'd bought her. But the way Cassandra kept her hand on her, kept her close as she guided her through the club, made it clear to everyone around them—Mia belonged to her.

Cassandra led her toward the back of the club and into another, smaller room. Inside, a crowd of people stood facing a stage at the end of the room. Mia couldn't see what was on it from so far back, but Cassandra parted the crowd and pulled her to the front.

"We're right on time. The show is just getting started." She guided Mia to stand in front of her. "Watch closely. I want your full attention on this."

Mia peered up at the stage. On it were two women, both dressed in lace corsets and thigh-high boots. The only difference between them was that one wore a thick leather collar around her neck.

Her submissive? She had to be.

Not a moment later, the Domme led her submissive to a large, wooden St. Andrew's cross at the center of the stage and began binding her to it with ropes. First her wrists, one after the other, at the top of the X. Then her ankles, her feet spread wide apart.

Then, from a table at the side of the stage, the woman produced a long, thin whip.

Mia's heart began to pound. She looked over her shoulder at Cassandra. Was this some kind of performance?

Cassandra reached up to Mia's cheek, turning her face back toward the stage. "Don't look at me. Keep your eyes on them."

Heat rose through Mia's body. Was it Cassandra's rebuke? Her touch? The silky smooth trill of her voice?

On the stage, the woman returned to stand by the cross. Using the handle of the whip, she turned her submissive's face toward her, kissing her with a tenderness that sent a visible tremor through the submissive's body.

Deep within Mia, desire ignited. While this may have been a performance, choreographed for the watching crowd, it wasn't an act. That kind of vulnerability couldn't be faked.

It was real. It was intimate. It was raw. The submissive was relinquishing control to the other woman, relinquishing her body, placing herself at her Domme's mercy.

Behind her, Cassandra leaned down, her lips brushing Mia's ear as she whispered, "Don't take your eyes off them."

Mia's breath caught in her chest. Enthralled by everything playing out before her, by Cassandra's voice, her presence, she couldn't move, couldn't speak. All she could do was watch as the woman on stage drew a hand down her submissive's arm, spoke softly into her ear. She still had the whip in her hand, and Mia was braced for what was to come.

Finally, the Domme stepped to the side. She raised her arm, pulling the whip back, then brought it down theatrically, snapping it against the woman's thigh with a loud crack.

Mia jolted. So did the woman on stage. But her Domme didn't falter, bringing the whip down over and over across the fronts of her thighs and her breasts. And with every strike, the bound woman's cries echoed through the room.

But they weren't cries of pain. No, they were cries of *ecstasy*.

Desire swelled in Mia's core, flooding her whole body. What would that feel like? Would it really feel *good*? If she closed her eyes, she could almost see herself bound to the cross in the woman's place...

"Do you see?" Cassandra slid her fingers down Mia's bare shoulder. "See how her body reacts to every impact? See how she anticipates the whip but doesn't fear it?"

Mia quivered. She could feel the heat radiating from Cassandra's body, feel the kiss of her breath on her neck. It was taking all of her strength not to crumble to pieces.

She drew in a steadying breath, focusing on the scene playing out on stage. While the woman continued to rain the whip down on her submissive's body, now and then she would communicate with her silently, with a touch, a whispered word. And the bound woman would respond with an inaudible murmur or a barely perceptible nod. She seemed drunk, on some other plane.

Cassandra's fingertips traveled down the back of Mia's

arm. "She's deep in subspace now. She's given in to sensation, to her Mistress, entrusting body and mind to her."

On stage, the Domme set the whip aside and brought her hand up to touch her submissive's cheek. The woman shuddered, her head rolling back as she fell deeper into her trance.

"See the way she looks at her?" Cassandra stepped in close, her body pressing against Mia's back. "Right now, her Mistress is her whole world. Right now, her Mistress is her *everything*."

A shiver rolled through Mia's body, Cassandra's words reverberating through her. She watched, entranced, as the Domme caressed her bound submissive, the woman's chest heaving with heavy breaths. She watched as the Domme's hand crept downward, further and further, until it slipped between the other woman's thighs. She watched as the Domme brought her submissive to heavenly release, right in front of the watching crowd.

She watched as the submissive thanked her Mistress for the privilege.

Mia's lips parted, a soft breath escaping from her. This was what Cassandra wanted from her. This was the surrender Cassandra desired.

"You've seen what you need to see," she said softly. "Come."

Mia turned to face her. She had a thousand thoughts running through her mind, a thousand feelings swirling in her body. She wanted to see more, feel more, immerse herself more deeply.

But the expression on Cassandra's face was resolute.

With a wistful glance at the stage, Mia turned and

followed her out of the room. But in her mind, the scene continued, with her on the cross in place of the submissive.

And in place of the woman holding the whip was Cassandra.

∼

They sat in near silence on the car ride home. But whenever Mia glanced at Cassandra next to her in the back seat, she caught Cassandra looking back at her, a look in her eyes that she couldn't decipher.

Mia turned back to the window, her heart thumping. What did that look mean? What had been the point of the entire night? After leaving the room with the stage, they'd wandered around the club, watching scene after scene play out, Cassandra instructing her to watch, observe. And all the while, Cassandra had been watching her.

Could it be that the trip to the club had been a test?

Had Mia passed it?

But Cassandra didn't seem inclined to share her verdict. It wasn't until they were back in the penthouse, the front door locked behind them, that Casandra spoke.

"It's getting late. You should go to bed."

That's it? Cassandra had dressed her up in a skimpy dress and lingerie, had taken her to a private club, and made her watch people do all kinds of kinky things right before her eyes.

And all she had to say was, *Go to bed*?

Cassandra folded her arms across her chest. "Is something wrong?"

Mia shook her head. "No."

"Now, Mia. If there's something on your mind, tell me."

"I mean it. There's nothing wrong. It's just that…" Mia glanced down at her feet. "I had a really good time tonight. I guess I don't want it to end."

Silence fell over them, the slow, rhythmic thrum of Mia's pulse in her ears the only sound she could hear. And her breath, growing heavier and heavier as Cassandra stepped toward her, closing the distance between them.

Slowly, she reached up to cup Mia's cheek. "There will be other nights. We have a whole month together, Mia. Believe me when I say I'm going to make the most of it."

Mia trembled. There was barely an inch between them. Could Cassandra feel the heat simmering inside her? Could she hear how Mia's heart had surged the moment she touched her?

"I have so much more to show you," Cassandra said softly. "So much for you to experience. All in due time. Just trust me."

Mia nodded. "I will. Thank you for tonight, *Mistress*."

That one little word lingered in the air between them. For a moment, neither of them moved or spoke. And Cassandra's eyes remained locked on Mia's, the intensity of her gaze hot enough to burn. But Mia couldn't look away. She was captivated.

Her hand still on Mia's cheek, Cassandra traced her thumb along her bottom lip.

"Mia," she whispered. "*Mine.*"

She pressed her lips to Mia's, a searing kiss that stole every last ounce of breath from her chest. Mia closed her eyes, need surging through her. While Cassandra's lips were soft and supple, her kiss was possessive, insistent, *hungry*.

A murmur rose from Mia's chest. Cassandra deepened the kiss, her lips growing more demanding, her hands falling to Mia's waist to pull her close. Mia dissolved into her body, yielding to her embrace, yielding to her will, until she was completely and utterly consumed by her.

She was Cassandra's. Cassandra was her world. Mia longed to give her the surrender she desired.

So when Cassandra broke away, it took all Mia's willpower to hold back her protest.

"Get some rest, okay?" Cassandra brushed Mia's hair behind her shoulder. "I'll see you tomorrow."

Mia nodded mutely. Without another word, Cassandra went into her bedroom and shut the door, leaving her standing alone in the living room.

She brought her hand up, tracing her fingers over her lips. The remnants of the kiss still lingered on them.

But it wasn't just a kiss. It was the answer Mia had been waiting for. She'd passed Cassandra's test. She'd shown her that she understood her role, proved herself worthy of it. The kiss? It was part reward, part Cassandra's way of branding Mia as her own.

Before tonight, she'd only been Cassandra's on paper. Now, their bond was sealed.

Mia floated into her bedroom. But as she prepared for bed, she knew she wouldn't be able to fall asleep.

Because the moment her head hit the pillow, her thoughts would be filled with Cassandra. Cassandra kissing her. Cassandra touching her. Cassandra *claiming* her. And so much more.

How long would it take for those thoughts to become reality?

CHAPTER 9

Mia watched the pot of pasta boiling away on the stove. She'd spent the afternoon grocery shopping before returning to the apartment to cook dinner.

Why was she bothering to cook when she could simply order anything she wanted, delivered to her door, all on Cassandra's dime? Because she needed something to do to take her mind off Cassandra.

But that was proving impossible. How was she supposed to stop thinking about Cassandra when she was living in her penthouse apartment, surrounded by luxury? How was she supposed to stop thinking about Cassandra after she took her to a BDSM club and made her watch all of her deepest, darkest fantasies play out before her eyes?

How was she supposed to stop thinking about the kiss they'd shared?

It had been unlike anything Mia had ever felt. She'd been kissed before, but not like that. Not with such hunger, such *need*. And the kiss had stirred the same in her—an insatiable desire for the woman she now called her Mistress.

Suddenly, everything between them felt very, very real.

On the stove, the pot of pasta boiled over, starchy water spilling across the stovetop. Mia cursed and turned off the burner, removing the pot from it and grabbing a nearby tea towel to mop up the mess.

She sighed. The whole point of cooking had been to take her mind off Cassandra, yet here she was, replaying the moment they'd kissed over and over in her mind. She needed to keep her imagination in check.

Because Cassandra had made herself clear. *I want a submissive, not a lover.* She didn't want intimacy. She didn't want romance, or any kind of emotional connection. She wanted a servant. Nothing more, nothing less. That was the point of their arrangement. It could never be anything real.

Mia grabbed a fork and pulled a strand of spaghetti from the pot. It was done. She poured out the water and tossed the pasta into the nearby frying pan, mixing it in with the other ingredients. She was making a simple carbonara that she'd cooked countless times before. She didn't dare try to cook anything more adventurous in an unfamiliar kitchen.

Plus, she'd made it to share with Cassandra. And since she'd grown up cooking for herself and her younger sister, it was the only thing in Mia's repertoire that she'd dream of serving to someone like Cassandra. Even then, it was nowhere near as sophisticated as what she was probably used to. And Mia couldn't hide how homemade it looked.

But based on the empty state of her fridge and cupboards, Cassandra rarely cooked for herself, so perhaps she'd simply appreciate a home-cooked meal. When was the last time she'd had one? She was obviously single, and the way she avoided speaking about her family left Mia wondering if she had anyone in her life who would do a simple thing like cooking dinner for her.

Not that Cassandra's personal life was any of her concern. Still, Mia couldn't help but wonder who her Mistress was underneath it all.

At the other end of the apartment, the front door opened. Cassandra was home.

Her stomach flipped. She hadn't seen Cassandra all day. She always left for work before Mia even woke up.

As she stirred the saucepan, Cassandra appeared in the entryway to the kitchen.

"Hi, Mistress," Mia said. "Welcome home."

Cassandra sauntered into the kitchen and looked around at the crowded countertops. "I see you've been keeping yourself busy."

"Yes." Mia turned off the burner and took the pot from the stove. "I made dinner for us."

"You didn't need to do that. I don't expect you to cook for me. If I wanted a maid, I would have hired one."

Mia's cheeks grew warm. "I know. I didn't do it because I thought I had to. I just wanted to." She glanced down at her feet, suddenly feeling stupid. "Besides, I had the free time. You said I should be available to you whenever, but I didn't know when you were going to be home, so…"

"Oh, Mia." Cassandra reached out, her fingertips brushing the bottom of Mia's chin. "While I appreciate your dedication, I should have been more clear about my expectations. I don't want you to sit around waiting for me whenever I'm gone. You may do whatever you please when I'm away. And I'll make sure to keep you apprised of my schedule from now on, okay?"

Mia nodded.

"As for dinner," Cassandra continued, "I was planning to order in, but I wouldn't want this food to go to waste."

"So you'll have some?" Mia asked.

"Of course. Let me get out of my work clothes first."

As she disappeared in the direction of the main bedroom, Mia dished out a serving of carbonara for each of them. Just as she finished setting everything on the dining table, Cassandra returned.

She took a seat. Mia joined her, watching with bated breath as Cassandra picked up her fork.

She twirled some pasta around it and took a bite, chewing thoughtfully. "Mm. This is good."

Mia beamed. "Thank you."

"I mean it. This is *delicious*."

Mia didn't miss the surprise in Cassandra's voice. "I've been cooking since I was a kid. Mom's a nurse's aide, so she works a lot, and at odd hours. So growing up, it was up to me to feed myself and my sister a lot of the time." She picked up her own fork and took a bite. The pasta was a little overcooked, but it was otherwise fine. "Actually, I wanted to ask you if I can go see my sister on Friday evening. I just want to make sure she's doing okay."

"Is something the matter?"

"No, I just want to check up on her. Make sure she's all right without me. She has Mom, of course, but she's always working."

Cassandra's brows drew together. "If I'd known you had obligations to your family, I would have made sure to take that into account when setting up our agreement."

"I don't. Like I said, I just want to check up on her."

Cassandra studied Mia's face. "Your sister. How old is she?"

"She's sixteen. Old enough to look after herself, I just worry sometimes." Mia shook her head. "I can catch up with her in the afternoon instead. I'll be back before you get home from work." Holly had a drama club meeting after school, so that would only give them an hour or so together, but that was better than nothing.

"It's fine. You may have the evening off."

"Thank you. I appreciate it."

But Cassandra didn't seem annoyed at Mia's request, or even disappointed. So why had she questioned it in the first place? Sure, she had the right to. Mia had agreed to make herself available to her at all times. Was it concern, then, that was behind Cassandra's questions?

It took her a moment to realize that Cassandra had spoken to her.

"Sorry, what was that?" Mia said sheepishly.

Cassandra gave her a firm look. "I said, after Friday, I expect you to be available to me all weekend, understood?"

"Yes. Sure."

"Good. Because once again, I have plans for us. Have you chosen a safe word yet?"

"Um, yes. It's *tiger*."

Cassandra nodded. Mia waited for her to continue. But instead, Cassandra picked up her fork and started eating again.

Mia's heart raced. What kind of wicked plans did Cassandra have for her this weekend?

Saturday couldn't come fast enough.

CHAPTER 10

Running late. I'll be there in 15.

Cassandra slid her phone back into her purse as she climbed the stairs leading up to the Queens Club. The building's majestic sandstone facade towered over her, but it was dwarfed by the modern skyscrapers surrounding it.

She pushed open the heavy wooden front doors and strode inside. She'd come here straight from work to meet with Riley, who claimed to have important news for her. But now, she had fifteen minutes to kill.

She headed for the club's bar. While she wasn't in the mood to socialize after a long day at work, as the owner of the Queens Club, making herself available to members was an important part of her role.

Or perhaps she was simply avoiding being alone with her thoughts. Because inevitably, they would fill with images of Mia.

Mia. Sweet Mia. Cassandra had taken her to Lilith's Den to see how she'd respond. And respond she had. Cassandra had seen the hunger in Mia's eyes as she looked up at the stage. She'd felt Mia shiver and squirm as she watched the two women.

She'd sensed the desire in Mia's voice when she thanked her Mistress at the end of the night.

And when Cassandra kissed her? An electric charge, a current of pure, unbridled need, had flooded her body until it was the only thing she could feel.

She could still feel it now. She could still taste those lips, could still feel Mia's body pressing back against hers, inviting Cassandra to devour her, the sweetest of forbidden fruit.

She reached the bar. It was still early in the evening, and there were only a few people in the room. One was Penelope, the club's newest member, who was sitting alone at a table nearby.

Cassandra ordered a drink, a vodka martini, and took it over to Penelope's table. "Mind if I join you?"

Penelope nodded. "Go ahead."

Cassandra set her drink down and took a seat across from her. "I'm glad to see you back here so soon. And after it took so long to get you to join the club in the first place."

"I had a free evening," Penelope said. "Thought I'd come see what this club was all about."

"That tour is still on offer, if you'd like. And I can introduce you to some of the other members."

"Thank you, but I'd rather take the time to explore everything for myself. And I've already met a few people here. You weren't lying about the club's membership. I wasn't expecting to share a drink with Amber Pryce tonight."

Cassandra peered over Penelope's shoulder to where the

Pryce family heiress and her bodyguard-turned-fiancée sat. Household names like Amber weren't uncommon at the Queens Club.

"She's roped me into some charity event of hers," Penelope continued. "But there are benefits to having a Pryce owe me a favor. And there are certainly benefits to this place. Lots of people to meet, new connections to be made."

Cassandra raised her glass. "To new friends." That was what the Queens Club was all about. Forming relationships, professional and personal. And Penelope seemed like the kind of woman Cassandra wanted to have in her corner, professionally *and* personally.

"To new friends," Penelope echoed.

They clinked their glasses together and drank.

"I owe you one for inviting me here," Penelope said. "I'd like to return the favor. I've moved into the resort space recently. It's my latest venture. Buying up old, failing resorts, transforming them into unique getaways. If you're ever in need of an escape, you're welcome to stay at any of them in exchange for some feedback on the experience."

"That's very generous of you."

"Well, there's one resort in particular I'd love for you to take on a test run." Penelope leaned in closer. "It's a beautiful old chateau hidden away in the mountains. Casa de la Diosa. For now, it's my own little private project, but I'm planning to eventually open it up to like-minded guests. You see, it's been outfitted with certain features that I'm sure a woman of your tastes would appreciate."

"And what tastes would those be?" Cassandra asked.

"The kind that led you and your… companion to Lilith's

Den the other night. I would have said hello, but I didn't want to interrupt."

This isn't the only exclusive club we're both part of. Penelope's words from the other day suddenly made sense.

But before either of them could speak, Cassandra's phone buzzed. It was a message from Riley. They were here.

"You'll have to excuse me," Cassandra said. "I need to speak with someone about an urgent matter."

Penelope nodded. "Don't forget about my offer."

Cassandra finished off what was left of her drink and headed to the elevator to meet Riley in her office on the top floor. Only she and Riley had access to the top floor of the club. There were only a few people in the world that Cassandra trusted, and Riley was one of them. She'd met them years ago when she hired them for a job. And after a few more jobs, she'd realized how useful Riley's skill set was and had offered them a Queens Club membership, along with occasional well-paid work. The money didn't matter to Riley, but the work did.

And over time, a friendship had developed between the two of them. Riley was the only person who truly knew who she was. Not because Cassandra had told them. She hadn't. And as far as she knew, Riley didn't know a thing about her past. But Cassandra got the sense that they'd picked up enough over the years to understand there was a darkness lurking there.

Was that because of their own past? Riley rarely spoke of their former career in the Special Forces, but Cassandra had done a thorough background check on them before hiring them for the first time. She'd read Riley's records, at least those that weren't classified. The fact that most of them *were* had told her all she needed to know.

Besides, Cassandra knew better than to dig too deep into the past. And Riley had left that life behind them. Nowadays, they worked as a private security contractor, mostly for Cassandra and other members of the Queens Club.

The elevator doors opened. Riley was already waiting for her outside her office at the end of the hallway. Cassandra greeted them as she unlocked the door and ushered them inside, shutting the door behind them. There was no one else on the floor, but she wasn't taking any chances.

"You have news for me?" she asked.

Riley nodded. "A security update from the team on your office. Diane was spotted near the building."

Cassandra's stomach iced over. Di had found her.

It had only been a matter of time. Cassandra's high-profile job meant she wasn't a hard woman to find. But what surprised her was that she hadn't heard a single thing from any of her contacts, legitimate or otherwise. Even her private investigator hadn't seen any sign of Diane. Had she been keeping a low profile, lurking in the shadows, waiting for the right time to pounce?

Cassandra leaned back against the front of her desk, crossing her arms. "When was this?"

"Today, around midday. She didn't try anything. She just walked by the building, stopped and took a look at the place. But when security realized it was her and made a move, she slipped away into the crowd."

Why had she gone to Cassandra's workplace? To scope

out the building? To find a way to get inside so she could confront Cassandra? No, it couldn't be that simple. It never was with Di.

"I want you to increase security at my office and my home," she said. "Keep your eyes peeled and tell your teams to do the same."

Riley nodded. "Understood."

But they didn't take the obvious cue to leave. Instead, they sat down on the chair in front of Cassandra's desk.

"So, after you told me about Diane," they said, "I looked her up. I wanted to know who I was dealing with, and I couldn't shake the feeling I knew her name somehow. Turns out, I was right."

They paused, giving Cassandra a chance to speak. But she remained silent.

Riley leaned forward, resting their elbows on their knees. "Diane Whiteford. Known as Belladonna in underworld circles. The media went crazy with her story. After all, it's not every day a wealthy philanthropist and model citizen is arrested for her involvement in shady dealings and ties to the criminal underworld. The long list of charges she faced included multiple counts of blackmail and extortion against high-profile individuals, including government officials. She got a 15-year sentence, but it was cut short by a few years on appeal. And now she's out."

"Now she's out," Cassandra echoed.

"So, what's your connection with her?"

"She… from a past life. One I'd prefer to forget."

Riley studied her face. "You're afraid of her."

"I'm not afraid of her," Cassandra said. "I'm afraid of what she's capable of."

"Why? What *is* she capable of?"

Cassandra rested her palms on the edge of the desk behind her. "Do you know why she's nicknamed *Belladonna*? It's a plant. It has beautiful flowers, enticing in shape and color. But the entire plant, including the flowers, contains a lethal poison. That's why it's known by another name. Deadly nightshade."

Understanding dawned on Riley's face. That was what Diane was. Seemingly innocuous. Beautiful, enticing, even. But she was toxic. Dangerous. Deadly, when she wanted to be.

Belladonna poisoned Cassandra all those years ago. Would Diane turn out to be lethal to her, too?

CHAPTER 11

Holly sucked her iced coffee through her straw with a loud slurp. "You should have seen Chelsea's face when I got the part. She was so mad! She already told everyone it was hers."

Mia nodded along, pushing the ice around in her plastic cup. Were her sister and Chelsea friends, or were they fighting again? She'd lost track.

"I don't know why she even cares," Holly said. "She only wants to be in the play because it will look good on her college applications. I mean, that's why I'm doing it too, but I actually like this stuff. I've been in drama club for years. She only joined a couple of months ago!"

"Uh-huh." Mia's gaze wandered around the coffee shop. It was filled with teenagers and college kids snapping selfies and photos of overpriced, sugary drinks that could barely be called coffee.

Mia had missed out on this part of her youth. She'd always been too busy. Working at the supermarket. Catching up on her schoolwork. Taking care of Holly.

She refocused her attention on her sister, who was still talking about the school play.

"It's just nice to be a part of something, you know?" she said. "I never bothered auditioning before because I wouldn't have been able to keep up with all the rehearsals. And I never knew when I was going to end up stuck in the hospital for weeks. I never got to do stuff like this. Being in plays. Joining sports teams. Even just going to parties. But now I can do all that."

Mia gave her a small smile. "Now you can." While it was too late for her to experience the carefree life of a teenager, it wasn't too late for her sister. "Just don't party too much. You need to keep your grades up to get into college."

Holly rolled her eyes. "Is there even any point? I'm not smart like you. My grades are never going to be good enough to get me any scholarships, and that's the only way we could afford it."

"Don't you worry about that. Just keep studying hard, and we'll find a way. Education is important."

"*You* didn't go to college."

Mia shrugged. "I had other priorities."

"You mean *me*."

"No, I mean our family."

Holly crossed her arms. "I'm not stupid. I know you didn't go to college because you had to take care of me."

"That's not why," Mia lied. But the truth was far too complicated. And being honest with her sister would only hurt her. "When I finished high school, it just didn't make sense for me to go to college, so I decided to put it off for a few years. You know, work for a bit, earn some money."

"Right, you just *decided* to work at a grocery store instead of going to college? Like I said, I'm not stupid. You didn't go because of *me*. You got a job instead because we were broke. We still are. And that's because of me, too."

"That's not—" Mia sighed. "Look, I'm not going to lie to you. You're not stupid, and you're old enough to understand how the world works. So sure, we don't have a lot of money, but that's not because of you. It's because our healthcare system is stupid and broken. That's *not* your fault, so don't blame yourself for it, okay? And don't *ever* feel like you're a burden."

"But—"

"What is it that Mom is always telling us? About what's important in life?"

"Family," Holly said.

"That's right. Family is what matters. *Love* is what matters. I love you. Mom loves you. And you're more important to us than all the money in the whole world."

"I guess," Holly mumbled. She stared down into her cup, stirring what was left of her drink with her straw. "Too bad *love* isn't going to send me to college."

"Well, not exactly. But you're *going* to college. We'll make it happen." Mia paused. Did she dare tell her sister about her agreement with Cassandra? She didn't have to share the details. "This job I'm doing? It pays really well. It's going to bring in enough for *both* of us to go to college."

Holly peered up at her. "Really?"

"Really."

"All that for being some rich woman's maid?"

Right, that was her cover story. "Yup."

"Wow. Must be some job."

You don't know the half of it. Mia looked at the time on her phone. "It's getting late. I need to take you home."

Holly grumbled a protest, but Mia ignored it. They finished off their drinks and headed out to the parking lot. Mia had driven them here in their mom's car, which she borrowed regularly. Cassandra had given her permission to use her car service whenever she wanted to go somewhere, but Mia didn't want to take advantage of her generosity. And while Holly would probably love being chauffeured around in an expensive car, it would draw too much attention for Mia's liking.

They made their way through the dimly lit parking lot. There were a few people scattered around, mostly teenagers. But there was one older man standing by a streetlight nearby, smoking a cigarette.

Mia slowed. *Is that... Bruno.*

Her pulse raced. He had to be here for her. How did he know where she was? Had he followed her?

Mia glanced around the parking lot. There were enough witnesses around to keep him from doing anything extreme. But the last thing she wanted was for Holly to get caught up in a confrontation with him.

She picked up the pace, urging her sister on. But Bruno had already spotted them. His dark eyes fixed on Mia, he tossed his cigarette to the ground, crushed it under the sole of his shoe, and began marching in their direction.

Shit. They were only a few feet from the car, but Bruno was seconds from reaching them. Mia couldn't run. She couldn't hide.

She had no choice but to face him.

Mia unlocked the car and turned to Holly. "Get in the

car and wait for me. I need to speak to someone." She glanced over her shoulder at Bruno. "And lock the door."

Her sister followed her gaze, finally noticing the man. He'd slowed his pace, but his menacing gaze was locked on Mia.

He wasn't going to let her get away.

"What's going on?" her sister asked.

"Just get in the car, Holly. *Now.*"

She did as she was told. Her sister safely inside the car, the doors locked, Mia steeled herself and turned, coming face to face with Bruno.

She stepped away from the car, attempting to put some distance between him and her sister. "What are you doing here?"

"You know why I'm here." Bruno's deep, gravelly voice sent dread rolling down Mia's spine. "I want my money."

Mia swallowed. "I'm working on it. I'll have it for you at the end of the month, just like I said."

"Why should I believe you?"

"Because I'm telling the truth. I'm working a job that will pay out at the end of the month. It'll be enough to cover everything I owe you. I just need a few more weeks."

Bruno's eyes narrowed. "I'm getting tired of waiting."

Mia's heart thumped harder. She resisted the urge to look back at the car. She didn't want to risk drawing attention to Holly. "I swear, I can get you the money. I just need a little more time."

Bruno folded his arms over his mile-wide chest. "I'm a reasonable man. So I'm going to give you one more chance. You have until the end of the month. But if I don't get the cash by then, it'll be out of my hands. And neither of us wants that to happen." He leaned in close, his cigarette breath suffocating her. "Because I might be a reasonable man. But my superiors? They don't share my patience."

Mia's stomach churned. This wasn't the first time he'd mentioned his superiors. Were they mafia? Something else?

"It won't come to that," she said. "I swear it."

"It better not. I'll be keeping an eye on you, *and* your family. Try anything funny, like running off or telling anyone, and that's it."

Mia nodded. "A-are we done here?"

Bruno straightened up. "For now. Next time I see you, it better be with my cash."

As he marched away, Mia let out the breath she was holding. Taking a few more breaths to gather herself, she returned to the car, sliding into the driver's seat and locking the doors.

"Mia?" Holly's voice trembled. "Is everything okay?"

Mia nodded. "Everything's fine. Let's get you home before Mom freaks out."

Mia started the car and pulled out of the parking lot, her hands gripping the steering wheel tightly. Bruno had given her until the end of the month, but could she trust the word of someone like him? What if he changed his mind? What if the 'superiors' he spoke of changed their minds? What if they came after her? And not only her, but her mom? Holly?

She pushed the thought to the back of her mind. She needed to focus on making it through the rest of the month. And she had no choice but to take Bruno at his word.

Because the alternative meant that her life and those of her loved ones were in danger.

CHAPTER 12

Cassandra looked up at Mia over the top of her newspaper. "Look who's finally awake."

Mia mumbled something wordless. She was *not* a morning person. It didn't help that she'd lain awake for hours last night, replaying her encounter with Bruno in her mind.

She rubbed her eyes, yawning. She'd forgotten that today was Saturday, which was why Cassandra wasn't at work like she usually was when Mia woke up. Instead, she was sitting on the couch sipping a cup of coffee as she read the newspaper.

The aroma of the coffee reached Mia's nose. *Coffee. That's what I need.*

She headed into the kitchen and poured herself a cup, leaning her elbows on the counter as she sipped it slowly, letting its warmth wake up her body. From her place at the counter, she had the perfect view of Cassandra sitting on the couch, framed by the cityscape outside the windows behind her. She was dressed in a robe of ivory-colored silk, and when she crossed her legs, Mia caught a flash of a bare thigh, pale, smooth, alluring—

"Make sure you eat some breakfast too," Cassandra said.

Mia blinked. "Hm?"

"We have plans today, remember? I can't have you exerting yourself on an empty stomach."

Mia's heart skipped. "Right. Yes, Mistress." She'd forgotten all about Cassandra's plans, too.

Mia waited for her to say more. Where was she taking her this time? Were they going back to Lilith's Den?

Would she finally get to serve her Mistress?

But Cassandra just set her newspaper down and drained what remained of her coffee. "I need to take care of some things in my study. I won't be more than an hour or so. Have breakfast, get dressed, and wait for me here."

Mia nodded. "What do you want me to wear?"

"Anything you like. We're staying in today." Cassandra rose from her seat. "I'll see you in an hour. Do not be late."

∽

Mia sat on the couch, fingers fidgeting in her lap. She'd been waiting for Cassandra for fifteen minutes, but she hadn't emerged from her study.

She'd done exactly as Cassandra instructed, eating a light breakfast and dressing in a casual but pretty skirt and top. While they weren't going out, she still wanted to look nice for her Mistress. And she liked to put a little extra effort into her appearance whenever Cassandra was around. It didn't feel right to wear jeans or sweats around a woman who always looked put together, even in her pajamas.

Finally, the study door opened. Mia rose to her feet as Cassandra entered the room. She was still in her robe, belted securely at the waist, her legs and feet bare. Her dark hair hung loose, not wild and untamed like Mia's but cascading down her shoulders in waves as silky as her robe.

Here Cassandra was, dressed for lounging around the house. And still, she was mesmerizing.

"I'm all done with my work," Cassandra said, joining her by the couch. "Now it's time for some *play*."

Mia's breath hitched. There was a gleam in Cassandra's eye that made her skin tingle and her body burn.

"I'm sure you're eager for more of what you saw the other night at Lilith's Den?"

"Yes, Mistress."

"Then let's get started." Cassandra turned to the coffee table beside them. "We have everything we need right here."

Mia glanced between Cassandra and the table. What did she mean by that?

Cassandra drew her hand over the dark wood tabletop. "I had this custom-made. And not just for the storage."

Mia examined the chest-like table. It had several drawers, but she'd never looked inside them. And as Cassandra glided her fingers over the table's edges, Mia noticed an O-ring attached to a corner. It wasn't the only one. There were a dozen identical rings attached all around the sides of the table.

Are those what I think they are? While Mia was inexperienced, she wasn't naive. How had she never noticed them before? How had she never realized what they were?

Cassandra rounded the table and opened up two drawers on the side of it. "Come. Take a look."

Mia peered into the drawers. What she saw inside sent heat rushing to her skin.

One drawer held a collection of whips, floggers, and riding crops. The other, a set of leather wrist and ankle cuffs and several coils of rope.

Cassandra reached into the drawer on the left and withdrew a single coil of rope. "Consider this an introduction to all the tantalizing delights your Mistress has in store for you."

Mia glanced at the rope in Cassandra's hands. Would she tie Mia up, torment her until she screamed in bliss, just like the woman on stage that night?

Would she then take what was rightfully hers?

Mia's stomach flipped. She longed to give herself to her Mistress in so many ways. But was she ready for *that*? She'd been more than willing to give up her virginity all along, but now that she was actually facing the possibility…

But Cassandra had made herself clear. *Only once I'm satisfied that you truly want it will I take what's mine.* Sex wasn't what she wanted from Mia. She wanted Mia's devotion. And Mia was eager to give it to her.

Cassandra unfurled the rope carefully. "What's your safe word?"

"It's… tiger," Mia replied.

"Good girl." Cassandra pointed to the end of the coffee table. "Kneel."

Obediently, Mia got to her knees at the end of the table, facing it. Ordering her to hold out her hands, Cassandra bound her wrists together with the rope, leaving a long tail free. Then she pulled Mia's wrists to the other end of the coffee table, tying the rope off to an iron ring at the table's end.

Cassandra tugged at the rope, testing her knots. "There. Nice and secure."

Mia's pulse quickened. While only her wrists were bound, with the top half of her body lying against the tabletop and her arms stretched up above her head, she could barely move.

She inhaled deeply, letting the rush of adrenaline, the thrill building deep in her center, overcome her anxiety. She could keep it together. She had everything under control.

At least, until Cassandra reached into the other drawer.

"I saw how much you enjoyed the show at Lilith's Den," she said. "I felt the way you quivered every time that whip hit."

Mia's cheeks grew hot. Had it been that obvious?

From the drawer, Cassandra produced a small leather flogger. "How about I give you a taste?"

Mia bit her lip. It was one thing to just watch. It was another to put herself at the mercy of another, to experience it for herself.

But she wanted to experience everything. The good. The bad. The divine. She wanted to know what it would feel like to be at the mercy of her Mistress.

She drew in a calming breath. "I'd like that, Mistress."

A slight smile crossed Cassandra's lips. "Let's make this a little more interesting."

Still holding the flogger in one hand, she reached into the drawer with her other hand, withdrawing a long leather riding crop.

She held both up before Mia. "I'll give you a choice. Which one?"

Mia glanced between the riding crop and the flogger. What was the point of giving her a choice when she was tied to the table, powerless to do anything at all? Was this some kind of test? A game?

"*Choose*," Cassandra said.

Mia nodded at the riding crop. "That one."

Cassandra returned the flogger to the drawer and slid it shut. "Excellent choice. A flogger might seem more intimidating, but something like this?" She caressed the slender leather tip of the crop with her fingers. "It has far more of a sting."

Mia swallowed.

"But don't you worry. I'm not going to push you past your limits. In fact, that's what this is all about."

She drew the tip of the riding crop up the back of Mia's thigh, dragging up the skirt of her dress on one side. A shiver shot up her leg and straight between her legs.

"I'm going to start slow," Cassandra said, tapping the riding crop against Mia's ass, "then ramp up the intensity. What I need you to do is tell me when you've reached the limits of what you can handle. *Mercy*. Whether it's after one lash or one hundred, when you've had enough, ask your Mistress for *mercy*. But no sooner, and no later. Understand?"

"Yes." But the word caught in her throat, emerging as little more than a squeak.

"Listen, Mia." Cassandra rounded the table to stand in front of her, leaning down and cradling Mia's chin in her fingers. "I'll be watching you closely to make sure I'm not pushing you beyond what you can handle. It's my responsibility to keep you safe, and I take that responsibility very seriously. But this kind of exploration can be dangerous, especially to someone as inexperienced as you. So it's also important for *you* to understand where your limits lie. You will be tempted to push them because it feels good, but you need to learn to listen to your body. That's what this is. A lesson in learning your own limits and enforcing them. Understand?"

Mia nodded. "Yes, Mistress."

Cassandra leaned over and kissed her, not deep and hungry like that night after Lilith's Den, but soft, gentle. Still, it was enough to make her heart race, her body tremble. Enough to snuff out all her anxieties. Enough to spark desire down between her thighs.

Cassandra broke away. "One last thing."

She pulled Mia's skirt up around her waist, exposing her thin cotton panties. And it wasn't just Cassandra she was exposed to. The floor-to-ceiling windows behind her would give anyone looking in a full view of the scene taking place inside. Could anyone see them this high up? Could anyone see *her*, bound to the table with her ass sticking out, Cassandra standing over her, riding crop in hand?

Why did the thought only make her hotter?

Cassandra positioned herself beside her. "Shall we begin?"

Mia held her breath, waiting for the inevitable. Would it hurt? That was the point, wasn't it? That was what made it so thrilling.

Not a moment later, Cassandra brought the riding crop down, a short, sharp tap against her ass. Mia's body jolted, more out of surprise than pain. It hardly hurt at all. Neither did the impact that followed.

Mia closed her eyes as Cassandra continued, slow, rhythmic taps on her ass cheeks and the backs of her thighs. But each tap was harder than the last. And soon, the taps turned to strikes that made her skin sting, even through her panties.

Another strike, harder again. Mia hissed through her teeth. That one hurt.

"Relax," Cassandra said above her. "Breathe. Listen to your body."

Relax? How am I supposed to relax right now?

But her Mistress had commanded it, so Mia had to obey. She rested her head on the table, taking deep breaths, feeling the coldness of the wooden tabletop against her chest, the side of her face, her arms. As the pain dissipated across her skin, it left a gentle burning in its wake.

And when Cassandra brought the crop down over her ass again, once, twice, three times, it ignited something in Mia's body, something deep, primal. A moan shook her, every part of her body flooding with adrenaline and endorphins.

And desire. Sizzling, *scorching* desire that ached even more than the skin on her ass and thighs did.

Cassandra slid the tip of the riding crop up the inside of Mia's thigh, sending electricity crackling through her. "Do you like the way this feels?"

Mia murmured something wordless, eliciting a sharp strike from the riding crop. It only inflamed her even more.

"When I ask you a question, I expect you to answer it," Cassandra said.

"Yes…" Mia spoke between breaths. "That feels… good." She could hardly believe it herself. Every part of her was crying out for *more*.

And her Mistress had no intention of letting up. As she struck Mia's ass and thighs, again and again, with ever-increasing intensity, Mia shuddered and gasped, drowning in the torrent of sensations Cassandra rained down upon her.

It was heaven. It was ecstasy. It was that space where the world slipped away, and her body slipped away, and there was nothing left but ecstasy.

A whimper spilled from her lips. She wanted to lose herself in this feeling, revel in it for as long as she could. But each strike of the crop was harder than the last, piercing through her blissful haze. And there was an unpleasant numbness creeping through her body that threatened to overwhelm her.

She gritted her teeth. *Mercy.* That was all she had to say. But she didn't want to stop. She didn't want to give in. If she could just push through…

No. Her Mistress had warned her about the dangers of pushing past her limits. She'd even told Mia that she would be tempted to do just that. But she needed to listen to her body.

"Mercy," she gasped. "Mercy."

The strikes stopped. And in the space of a heartbeat, Cassandra's hands were on Mia's cheeks, cradling her face.

"It's over," she said. "You did wonderfully."

Mia trembled. The skin of her thighs and ass ached from the riding crop. But more than that, she ached for her Mistress's touch.

"You're all right," she said. "I'll untie you, then it's time for aftercare, okay?"

Mia nodded. Cassandra unbound her wrists and pulled her to her feet, drawing her into a deep, reassuring kiss. Mia pressed her body against Cassandra's, clutching onto her tightly. She wanted more from her. More than Cassandra's touch, her lips. More than Cassandra's body against hers. She wanted Cassandra to quench the embers smoldering in her core.

Instead, she broke off the kiss and pulled Mia over to the couch, drawing her down to lie across it, her head in Cassandra's lap. As she stroked Mia's hair with one hand, the other reached down to caress Mia's burning thighs and ass cheeks.

Mia purred. Cassandra's fingers soothed her tender, raw skin, her touch near such sensitive places making Mia throb between her thighs. She was still wearing her panties, but the cotton was so thin it was barely there.

She shifted in Cassandra's lap, the need within her becoming too much to bear. "Mistress," she pleaded.

Cassandra shook her head. "Not yet. You're not ready."

Mia sighed, frustration and relief warring inside her. She wanted Cassandra so badly. At least, her body did.

But her mind? Her heart? When she put herself up for auction, she'd had no hesitations about giving her body up to a stranger. But now, a part of her wondered—did she want more from her first time than just a few moments of gratification?

But she was in no state to untangle those thoughts. So she closed her eyes, savoring her Mistress's touch, ignoring the throbbing inside her.

"All in due time," Cassandra said softly. "All in due time."

But time was the one thing the two of them didn't have. This arrangement of theirs had an expiration date. Mia couldn't forget that. She couldn't let herself fall too deeply under Cassandra's exquisite spell.

No matter how much she wanted to.

CHAPTER 13

Cassandra shifted slightly on the couch, taking care not to disturb Mia in her lap. She was so still and silent that Cassandra couldn't tell whether she'd fallen asleep. How long had they been lying there, basking in the sunlight streaming through the windows, the warmth of each other's bodies?

She stroked her fingers up Mia's arm gently, over the faint freckles scattered across her skin like stars. The feel of her soft skin under Cassandra's fingertips was just as intoxicating as the sweet floral scent of her hair, the press of her against her body. And her lips. Those sweet, inviting lips…

Everything about her was irresistible. It had taken all of Cassandra's willpower to hold herself back when Mia begged her to take things further. That whimpered *'Mistress'* had stirred every desire within her. And in that moment, she'd wanted nothing more than to take Mia right there on the couch.

But reason had won out. She'd resisted. It was the hardest thing she'd ever done.

Mia stirred in her lap, a murmur rising from her chest. "God, that feels good. I want to lie here forever."

"We can lie here a little longer," Cassandra said. "But then I need to get you some water. And something to eat. You pushed yourself hard, and I'm proud of you for it. But you need to replenish your body, understand?"

Mia's cheeks turned pink. "Okay."

"Is something the matter?"

"It's just that I'm not used to this. Having someone telling me to take care of myself all the time."

"Is it a problem?"

Mia shook her head. "It doesn't bother me. It's actually kind of... nice." The flush on her cheeks deepened. "I've never had anyone looking out for me like that. I've always had to take care of myself, even when I was a little kid."

"What about your mom?"

"Mom had her hands full with her job and Holly. I started helping out with Holly as soon as I was old enough, too. I'm practically her second mom."

"I'm sorry," Cassandra said. "You didn't deserve that. You deserved to have someone to look after you, too."

"Don't get the wrong idea. I wasn't neglected or anything. Mom always made sure I had everything I needed. I always felt loved and cared for. I just had to grow up a little faster than most kids."

There was no bitterness in Mia's voice as she spoke those words, but Cassandra could feel the weight behind them, could feel how much of herself Mia had sacrificed for her family.

"But it was all for my sister," Mia said. "So she could have some semblance of a life. That made it all worthwhile."

"What about *your* life?" Cassandra asked. "Didn't you deserve to have a life of your own instead of always putting your sister first?"

"Maybe. But even if I could, I wouldn't change anything. Besides, that's all in the past. Holly can take care of herself now. But it's kind of hard not to feel like I still have to look after her."

"I understand. You love her. And old habits are hard to break."

Mia nodded. "I've just spent so much of my life being responsible for her. With my mom working all the time, it was on me to hold our family together. I was the one making sure all the bills got paid. I was the one keeping track of all of Holly's appointments. I was the one helping her when she fell behind at school…"

Mia's gaze grew distant. "This might sound silly, but I think maybe that's what draws me to all this. You know, this idea of giving up control. Sometimes, I just feel like I'm drowning in everything. All my worries. All my responsibilities. So being able to let go of my responsibilities and give someone else the reins? It's so… liberating."

Cassandra leaned down and kissed her on the forehead. "Then it's fortunate that life brought us together. With me, you don't have to worry about a thing."

Mia closed her eyes, sighing softly. "I can't even tell you how much that means to me. I know this is just temporary, but it's nice to escape it all, if only for a little while."

Just temporary. Mia was right. What was between them couldn't last. But was there any harm in indulging in it?

"What if you could truly escape?" Cassandra asked.

"What if you could start fresh, free from any responsibilities? What would you do?"

Mia's brows crinkled. "I don't know. I've never thought about it before. I've never really had any options other than the path my life has always been on."

"Don't you have any dreams? Places you want to go, things you want to do, to be?"

"Not really. There's college, I guess. I feel like I missed out in that department. I was supposed to go after high school, actually. I've never told anyone this, but I got a scholarship to go to a school across the country. But that would have meant…"

"Moving away from your family?"

Mia nodded. "Holly was only 13 at the time and was at the top of the list for a heart transplant. And after the surgery, she'd need months of recovery. There was no way Mom could look after her all by herself while still working enough to keep us afloat. I had to help. So I turned the scholarship down. I didn't even tell Mom about it because I knew she'd try to make me go. I just got a job at the grocery store, and I've been working there ever since. I figured college, a career, my dreams—none of that mattered, as long as I had my family." She glanced up at Cassandra. "Is that sad? That I can't even dream of a life that doesn't revolve around them?"

"No. All that means is you have a caring, selfless heart." Cassandra brushed her thumb along the side of Mia's chin. "But be careful. If all you do is give, soon there won't be anything left."

As silence fell over them, Mia seemed to wrestle with

Cassandra's words. Here was a woman so accustomed to sacrifice that she'd never given her own needs a second thought.

But Cassandra had sensed that in Mia from the very beginning. The way she hesitated at Cassandra's offers of clothes and gifts, as if the very idea of being given anything lavish was incomprehensible. The way she was so quick to dismiss any suggestion that her life of putting her family first had been difficult. The way she was determined to serve Cassandra in ways that went beyond what was written in their contract, like making her home-cooked meals.

Mia was always putting others before herself. When was the last time Cassandra thought about anyone's needs but her own? Most of her relationships were built on give and take, on favors and transactions. Were any built on generosity, on trust?

But trusting others was a risk. Most people weren't like Mia. Most people were only ever out for themselves. Which meant Cassandra had to look out for herself and herself alone.

Mia broke the silence. "What about you? If you could start fresh, what would you do?"

"I don't need to start fresh," Cassandra said. "I've already built the life that I want for myself. And I've already started over twice before."

"You have?"

Cassandra stretched one arm across the back of the couch, the other falling down to rest on Mia's shoulder. "The first time was when I was seventeen. My family situation had gotten difficult, so I ran away from home to escape it. Got on a bus across the country and didn't look back."

"Oh. I'm sorry."

"Don't be. Despite everything, I was able to keep a roof over my head, to stay fed and warm. I was one of the lucky ones." At least, that was what Cassandra told herself.

"What about the second time?" Mia asked. "You said you started over twice."

"The second time? I ran away to escape something worse."

And now, that *something* had caught up with her.

Mia peered up at her, waiting for her to elaborate.

Instead, she eased Mia up from her lap. "But that's enough talk. You need to eat and drink something." She rose to her feet. "Stay right there."

But as Cassandra went into the kitchen and poured her a glass of water, she could still see Mia looking back at her, pity in her eyes. Was it pity, or understanding? Could someone like Mia ever understand what Cassandra had been through, the life she'd lived? Could she understand the desperate measures people went through to survive?

Perhaps Cassandra had underestimated her. After all, she'd gone as far as to auction off her virginity. And there was more to Mia's story than she was letting on. Cassandra knew it.

Yes, there was more to her than that wisp of a young woman who trembled and stammered in Cassandra's presence the first time they met. Perhaps she'd been wrong in assuming Mia was a naive girl, one who needed saving.

But that didn't stop Cassandra from wanting to save her.

Because Mia needed someone looking out for her. Just like Cassandra had needed someone back then.

Could being that person for Mia quell the ghosts of Cassandra's past?

CHAPTER 14

Mia took a seat on the couch and set her cup of coffee on the table. It was the same table Cassandra had tied her to just days earlier before spanking her with a riding crop and leaving her desperate and aching.

The worst part? Mia couldn't do anything to relieve that ache. Not even by herself.

The submissive's body belongs to her Dominant. She will not pleasure herself in any way. When she signed the contract, she hadn't expected that to be the hardest clause to deal with. Yet here she was, longing for the sweet release she'd been denied for what felt like an eternity.

How many days had it been since she signed that contract? How many days since they met at that club, and Cassandra spoke the words, *"Before the month ends, you'll be begging me to take you"*?

Mia had done everything *but* beg. And Cassandra wouldn't touch her. Not in the way Mia wanted her to.

The front door to the penthouse opened. *Speak of the devil.* Cassandra stepped into the room, looking enthralling as ever, despite having spent the last ten hours at work. But maybe that was Mia's current state of denial talking.

Remembering herself, she got to her feet. "Good evening, Mistress."

"Good evening." Cassandra slipped off her heels and hung up her coat, then wandered over to the couch, collapsing onto it. "Is that dinner I smell? I'm famished. I haven't had a spare moment to eat all day."

"Dinner is in the oven," Mia said. "It should be ready in half an hour."

"Wonderful. It smells delicious." She looked Mia up and down. "Almost as good as you look. I adore that dress on you."

"Thank you, Mistress." Even Mia had to admit that the royal blue shift dress, cinched at the waist with a gold belt, looked good on her. Cassandra had bought it for her the day before, along with a dozen other new outfits, all so she could pick and choose what Mia wore for her every single day. She seemed to take pleasure in controlling the minutiae of Mia's everyday life. While Mia should have found it stifling, instead, she found it freeing.

Cassandra patted the seat next to her. "Sit."

Mia obeyed.

Cassandra leaned back on the couch with a sigh. "I can't deny I'm enjoying having you cook for me. Among... other things."

She slid her hand up the front of Mia's thigh. Mia exhaled slowly. She was so on edge that a single touch was enough to make her throb between her legs.

"I'm at your service," she whispered, "*Mistress.*"

Had Mia started calling her Mistress instead of her

name in an attempt to seduce her into making a move? Maybe. Was it working? No.

At least, not yet.

Cassandra glanced toward the kitchen, her hand still on Mia's thigh. "Half an hour until dinner, you said?"

Mia nodded.

"Perhaps you can keep me entertained until then."

She reached up and drew Mia's face to hers. But before their lips could meet, Mia's phone began buzzing furiously on the table beside them.

Mia cursed internally. But when she glanced at her phone, her irritation turned to concern. "It's my mom."

Cassandra sat back. "Do you need to take it?"

Mia shook her head. "But maybe I should. It could be something to do with Holly. Mom usually just texts me unless it's an emergency."

"Go on. Answer it."

Mia picked up her phone. "Hi, Mom."

The voice at the other end of the line was stern and sharp. "I need you at the house. We need to talk."

Mia's heart sank. "What's going on? Is it Holly? Is she okay?"

"Holly's fine. But you need to come home right now."

"I don't understand."

"Just come home, Mia," her mom said. "This is important."

"Okay. I'll see what I can do."

Mia hung up the phone, her hands shaking slightly. What had her mom so worried?

Cassandra placed her hand on Mia's. "Is everything all right?"

"I don't know. My mom wants me to come home, but she won't say why. She sounded so serious."

"Then you better go see what it's about."

"Is that okay? Our agreement says I'm supposed to—"

Cassandra held up her hand. "Our agreement doesn't matter. I'm telling you to go. I can come with you if you'd like."

Mia shook her head. "That's okay." Having to explain Cassandra's presence to her mom would only complicate things.

Cassandra rose to her feet. "I'll call a car. It will take you there and wait for you until you're ready to return. If you need to stay more than a few hours, let me know."

Mia nodded. "Okay. Thank you."

But as she readied herself to leave, she couldn't ignore the part of her that wished Cassandra was coming too.

˜

The car pulled up in front of Mia's family home. Without waiting for the driver to open her door, she got out of the car and dashed up to the house. Her mother stood outside the front door waiting for her, concern written in the lines of her face.

"Is everything okay?" Mia asked. "Where's Holly?

"At a rehearsal for the school play." Her mom warily eyed the car parked by the curb. "What's all this?"

"My boss called a car to bring me here. What's going on?"

Her mom tipped her head toward the house. "Come inside first."

She ushered Mia into the house, scanning the street outside carefully before closing the door behind them. Then she led Mia into the living room, away from the door and windows.

"What's going on?" Mia said. "Why are you acting all paranoid?"

"You tell me." Her mom crossed her arms. "Mia, what have you gotten yourself into?"

"You mean my job? I told you, it's—"

"As shady as this job of yours sounds, that's not what I'm talking about. I'm talking about the man who keeps driving past our house at all hours of the day and night, watching us."

Mia's stomach dropped. "What man?"

But she already knew the answer. *I'll be keeping an eye on you, and your family.* It could only be Bruno.

"Again, you tell me," her mother said. "He told me you know him."

"What? You talked to him?"

"I sure did. I'd had enough of him creeping about, so when he drove past this afternoon, I went out to confront him. When I asked him who he was and what he was doing, he told me he's a friend of yours and I should talk to you about it. I told him if I caught him lurking outside my house again, there'd be hell to pay."

"You did *what?*"

Her mom put her hands on her hips. "Who is he, Mia? What's going on?"

Mia shook her head. "It's nothing. Nothing I can't handle."

"Mia Jacqueline Brooks. *Do not* lie to me."

"I'm not lying. I have it under control."

"Then you'll have no problem telling me what's going on. Talk to me, honey. Who is this guy? Is he a boyfriend? An ex?"

Mia cringed. "You think he's my *boyfriend*?"

"I know he's a lot older than you, but these things happen. And older men can take advantage—"

"Mom, no. I promise you, it's *nothing* like that."

"Then what's going on?"

Mia sighed. "It's a really long story."

"And I've got all the time in the world." She led Mia to the couch and pointed at the seat. "So start talking."

Drawing in a deep breath, Mia sat down. "The man you talked to? His name is Bruno. A coworker introduced me to him a few years ago. I don't know if you remember, but back then, money was *really* tight. It was right after Holly had her transplant, and with you cutting back on your shifts so you could take care of her, we were struggling to pay the bills. I wanted to help. My coworker overheard me begging for extra shifts and told me she knew someone who could help me out with my money problems."

Mia had been barely out of high school at the time, and too naive for her own good. She didn't know what a loan shark was. All she saw was someone who could give her a lifeline. It hadn't occurred to her that no one in their right mind would loan money to an eighteen-year-old making minimum wage with no credit score. No one legit, anyway.

"He set me up with a loan, just a few hundred dollars. Enough to cover groceries and bills for the month. I paid it back quickly, so I borrowed a little more for the next month. Just to help take some of the pressure off."

"Wait." Her mom's eyes narrowed. "I remember that. You said that money was from picking up extra shifts at the store."

"I know. I lied. I didn't want you to worry. And I thought I had it under control. Because I did, at first. But then everything just snowballed, and the debts started to pile up."

Of course, the exorbitant interest Bruno tacked on hadn't helped. It had taken Mia far too long to see the red flags. But by then, she was in too deep. By then, she owed more money than she could ever pay back.

"Eventually, I stopped borrowing money from him, but as soon as I did, he got hostile. He demanded that I pay everything back immediately."

That was when the threats started. While Bruno had always been vague about what would happen if she didn't pay him back, it was obvious he had connections to people far more dangerous and powerful than himself.

She'd had no one to turn to for help. And that coworker who had told her about him?

She'd simply disappeared one day, never to be seen again.

But her mom didn't need to know that. She didn't need to know about the threats. Mia didn't want her worrying more than she already was.

"But like I told you, I have it all under control," Mia said. "This job I'm doing, it'll give me enough money to cover everything I owe and more. I get paid at the end of the month, and Bruno said I can pay him back then. After that, this will all be over. He won't give us any more trouble."

She peered up at her mom, bracing herself for the inevitable tongue-lashing. After all, she deserved it.

Instead, her mom sat down next to her and put her arms around her, pulling her into a hug.

"Oh, honey…" Her voice quavered. "I'm sorry. This is all my fault."

Mia drew back. "No, it's not. I'm the one who took out the loans. It was stupid of me."

"But you did it for us. I should have never made you feel like it was your responsibility to take care of the family. That's my job, not yours."

"I just wanted to help. I could see how bad things had gotten, how much you were struggling. I had to do *something*."

"No, you didn't. I would have managed, like always."

"You say that, but you were drowning, Mom! Holly was too young to see it, but I wasn't. You think I didn't notice all the meals you skipped? You always said you'd grab something on your way to work, but you never left home early enough to stop anywhere before your shift started. You wore all your clothes and shoes until they were falling apart. And all those days you went with only a few hours of sleep until you could barely stand?"

"Those choices were mine alone," her mom said. "They had nothing to do with you."

"Yes, they did. I could feel how close to the edge we were. I saw all the bills piling up. We couldn't keep living like that. *You* couldn't keep living like that."

"I would have found a way. I would have done anything to keep you girls safe. Anything to protect you from things like this! Mia, this man, this Bruno. He's a loan shark! He's dangerous. You know how people like him operate, don't you?"

"I know. But I'm going to pay him back. This will all be over at the end of the month."

"Right, because of this job of yours? You understand why I'm skeptical, don't you? It sounds too good to be true."

"I know. But it *is* true." Mia took her mom's hands in her own. "Life has given us a break, just this once. Soon, I'm going to have enough money to pay off all our debts and more. Just trust me."

"*Fine*. I'll trust that you can handle this. But if this Bruno character gives you any more trouble, tell me. We can go to the police, or find some other way to deal with it, okay?"

Mia nodded. "Okay."

Her mom sat back. "God, when did this all happen? It feels like it was only last year that I was teaching you how to tie your shoelaces. But you're all grown up now." She let out a heavy sigh. "No, you've been grown up for a long time. You had to grow up too fast. That wasn't fair to you, and I'm sorry."

"It's okay. It just made me good at taking care of myself. It made me strong. You don't have to worry about me."

"I wish that were true. You're my daughter. I'll always worry about you. You have no idea how stressed out I've been, sitting here wondering what kind of mess you got yourself into with that man."

Mia shook her head. "I can't believe you thought Bruno was my boyfriend. Seriously? You think I'd date someone like *him*?"

"Well, it's not like you ever tell me about the guys you're dating," her mom muttered.

"Because there's never been anything to tell. I've never

even had a boyfriend. *Or* a girlfriend. Because I like women too."

"Oh." Her mother paused. "That's great, honey!"

"Actually, I think it's more that I don't care about whether someone's a man or a woman. I don't know how to explain it. Honestly, I haven't given this much thought until recently."

Her mom cocked her head. "Did you meet someone?"

"Kind of. It's nothing serious. It's more of a fling. But… I just can't stop thinking about her. I get butterflies around her. And when she kisses me—" Mia stopped short. Her mom did *not* need to know about the kind of things she felt when Cassandra kissed her. "But like I said. It's just a fling."

"I don't know. That sounds pretty serious to me. And whoever this woman is, she'd be lucky to have you."

"Thanks, Mom."

She patted Mia on the leg. "I'm just happy to see you smiling about someone like this. I'm sure your dad would be too. And you know, I always wanted another daughter, so if I end up with a daughter-in-law—"

"Mom!"

"Okay, okay." She pulled her hand away. "It's almost dinnertime. Do you want something? I have to get ready for work soon, but I can heat up some leftovers."

"Thanks, but I should get going." The dinner she'd cooked was waiting for her back in the apartment. She'd told Cassandra when to take it out of the oven before she left.

Her mom led her to the door and pulled her into a smothering hug, not letting go until Mia slid from her grasp.

"I need to go," she said. "But I'll talk to you soon."

"All right. And remember, this place will always be your home. You can come back here whenever you want." Her mom looked her up and down. "What is this you're wearing?"

Right, the dress. "It was on sale," Mia lied. She was *not* explaining to her mom that her 'employer' liked to dress her up in expensive clothes. "Just thought I'd try a new look."

"Huh. Well, I like it. It's nice to see you in something other than jeans."

Mia said goodbye and headed down to the car where the driver waited, holding the back door open for her. As she slid into the back seat, she pulled her phone from her purse. She had a message from Cassandra.

Did you make it home? Is everything all right?

Everything's fine. Just some family stuff. I'm on my way back now, she sent back.

I'm glad. See you soon.

Mia set her phone down in her lap, warmth swelling in her chest. Was Cassandra's concern simple politeness, or was it genuine? It was hard to tell with her. She rarely let her emotions show, always projecting an inscrutable facade.

At least, that was how it had seemed at first. But in the days since, Mia had caught glimpses of her softer side, and the lines between 'Cassandra' and 'her Mistress' had started to blur. Was the way Cassandra worried about her, doted over her, all just part of her duty as her Domme, or was it more?

But the bigger question on Mia's mind was how *she* felt about Cassandra. Because while their relationship had been defined by a month-long contract, there was a connection between them that Mia felt even when they were apart.

Was it just a side effect of the kinky games they were playing?

Or was it something real?

CHAPTER 15

"What do you think?"

"Hm?" Mia looked up at Cassandra. It was early in the evening, and the two of them were lounging in the living room, Cassandra on the couch, Mia sitting on the rug at her feet, her back against it. She'd been scrolling lazily through her phone while Cassandra worked away on her laptop, but apparently, she'd stopped to ask Mia something.

But Mia hadn't heard a word she'd said. She had too much on her mind. Bruno. Her mom. Her increasingly complicated feelings for her Mistress.

Who was staring down at her, awaiting an answer.

"Um..."

"Were you listening to me at all?" Cassandra asked.

"I'm sorry," Mia said quickly. "I was distracted."

Cassandra studied her face. "Is everything all right?"

"It's fine. I just have a lot on my mind."

"Is this about the other day? With your mother?"

Mia nodded. "But like I said, it's fine."

"Whatever it is, if it's bothering you this much, it's *not* fine. Don't think I haven't noticed how preoccupied you've been these past few days. When your mind is elsewhere, you're not here with me, and we can't have that, can we?"

Mia looked down at her lap. "I'm sorry, Mistress."

"Don't apologize. Tell me what's wrong."

"It's… complicated."

Cassandra shut her laptop and placed it on the table beside her, then slid down onto the floor to sit next to Mia, her legs folded to one side. "Go on. I'm listening."

"Well, I told you why I decided to do this. You know, auction myself off. But I didn't tell you everything…"

Before Mia knew it, she was spilling it all to Cassandra. About her family. About how her sister's medical bills had sent them deep into debt. About how she'd gone to a loan shark in secret to help out with their money problems. About how Bruno had started threatening her, and her mom had found out the truth.

About how she now owed him so much money that she'd resorted to selling her virginity.

All the while, Cassandra listened silently, her face stone.

"But once I get the money, I'll be able to pay him off," Mia said. "And it'll all be over."

"How much?" Cassandra said firmly. "How much do you owe him?"

"I don't even know anymore. With all the interest, it has to be six figures by now."

"That's *extortionate*."

"Maybe. But Bruno isn't the type to care."

"Oh, believe me, I'm familiar with his type." Cassandra's voice dripped with venom. But it softened as she put her hand on Mia's arm. "Let me help you. I'll make a few calls, get this 'Bruno' off your back."

Mia shook her head. "No. You can't go to the police. That'll only make things worse."

"Who said anything about the police?"

Mia stared at her. What did that mean? "Look, I don't want you getting involved with someone like him."

"Like I said, I know his type. I've dealt with far worse."

Mia shook her head again. "Still, I don't want your help with this. Or anyone else's. It's nothing personal. I just want to handle this myself."

"Are you sure? Do you truly understand the position you're in?"

Mia nodded. "Yes. And I'm handling it. Bruno gave me until the end of the month. He promised me that. As long as I have the money by then, everything will be fine."

"And you *will* get it. I'm a woman of my word. I'll keep up my end of our agreement. And in the meantime, if anything changes at all, let me know. If Bruno threatens you again, tell me immediately. I'll make sure he doesn't come near you ever again."

Mia nodded. But how would Cassandra even do that? Something told her that she didn't want to know.

"Now, come here." Cassandra wrapped an arm around her, drawing her close. "Thank you for telling me that. It's important that I'm aware of everything that's going on with you. Whether or not it affects me, it's my job to look after your well-being, understand?"

"Yes, Mistress."

"Good girl."

Cassandra planted a kiss on Mia's lips. It was soft and gentle, yet it sent desire surging through her, stronger than ever before. Cassandra was still denying her any release, from her hand or Mia's own.

A whimper spilled from her lips. She pulled away, her whole body alight. Could her Mistress see how hot just a single kiss had made her? Could she see how pathetically, desperately aroused she was?

"What's the matter?" Cassandra asked.

"Nothing!" The truth was far too embarrassing to admit.

"I don't believe you one bit. Come on now. What's the problem? Tell me."

Mia sighed. "Well, it's just that, since this month started, I haven't been able to…"

"Yes?"

"To… you know." She glanced away, her cheeks burning. "I usually take care of myself a few times a week, but now I can't. And you keep getting me all worked up, and I can't do anything about it—"

"Oh? So this is my fault?"

"No! But whenever you kiss me, it gets me all flustered…"

A smile pulled at the corners of Cassandra's lips. "You mean when I do this?"

She leaned in and pressed her lips to Mia's again, harder this time, more demanding. Mia let out a low murmur, need flaring inside her. Cassandra deepened the kiss, her body pushing against Mia's, her hand sliding up the side of Mia's thigh, up her stomach, fingers teasing the side of her breast—

"Mm, yes…" Mia pried herself away again. "When you do that. It's like torture. I can't take any more of this, Mistress!"

"Oh, you poor thing." Cassandra traced her thumb along the curve of Mia's chin. "Honestly, I've been waiting to see how long it would take for you to crack. I know you've been trying so hard not to."

Mia blinked. So Cassandra had noticed? And she was getting Mia all worked up on purpose like it was some kind of game?

"You lasted far longer than I expected," Cassandra said. "And without a single complaint. I think you deserve a reward."

Mia bit her lip. "A reward?"

"That's right. Something that will relieve a little of this… *tension*." She rose to her feet, beckoning Mia with a finger. "Come with me."

Mia stood up and followed her Mistress. Where was she taking her?

But the answer became clear when they reached the main bedroom. *Cassandra's* bedroom.

The door was already open a crack. Cassandra pushed it open all the way and led her into the room. Mia hadn't been inside it before, only catching glimpses of it when she walked by. The bed was even bigger than the one in Mia's bedroom, and unlike in her room and the rest of the house, there were personal touches here and there. A book on the nightstand. A throw blanket on the armchair next to it. Artworks on the walls depicting abstract female forms.

"Get onto the bed for me," Cassandra said.

Mia's heart skipped. "You want me to…"

"Don't make me repeat myself. Do you want your reward or not?"

Mia glanced between Cassandra and the bed. Was her Mistress finally going to take what she'd "bought" from her in the first place?

No, not when Mia hadn't asked her to. And not with so little fanfare. This was something else.

She walked over to the bed and climbed onto it. The sheets were pure white silk, the pillows soft as clouds. As she lay down on her back, propping herself up on her forearms, Cassandra swept her eyes along Mia's body from head to toe, taking in the sight of her displayed on the bed. Her skin sizzled under her Mistress's searing gaze, but she resisted the urge to shield herself from it, instead waiting obediently for her next command.

And when Cassandra finally spoke, it was with a deep, seductive voice that sent a shiver through Mia's body.

"Take off your panties."

Skin tingling in anticipation, Mia reached under her skirt and raised her hips off the bed, peeling her panties down her legs.

"Sit back against the pillows," her Mistress ordered.

Mia did as she was told. Cassandra seated herself at the edge of the bed, turning her body to face Mia.

"Pull up your skirt for me," she said.

Mia drew her skirt up around her waist, her knees together. She already knew what Cassandra's next command would be.

"Spread your legs."

Mia's pulse quickened. Once again, she obeyed.

"Good girl." Cassandra brushed her fingers up the inside of Mia's calf with a feather-light touch. "Now, about that reward. I'm going to let you release some of that tension yourself."

Mia's lips parted silently. Did she want Mia to touch herself while she watched? And on *Cassandra's bed*?

"Go on. Show me how you—how did you put it? *Take care of yourself*." She slid her hand up to Mia's knee. "Show me how you like to be touched."

Mia hesitated. While she didn't feel any shame about pleasuring herself, having someone watch her do it was another matter. It seemed so indecent. So intimate.

So thrilling.

She drew in a breath and shut her eyes, running her hand down her stomach—

"No," Cassandra said. "Don't close your eyes. Look at me."

She opened her eyes. Cassandra's gaze was locked on hers, a wordless command that she was powerless to resist. And after days of denial, Mia's need drowned out any hesitation.

Slowly, she slipped a hand down between her legs. She was slick and warm, already dripping wet. She slid her fingers up and down, over her folds, over her entrance, before dragging them up to her swollen clit.

A murmur rose from her chest. It had been so long, and she was so hypersensitive that the lightest of touches sent pleasure sparking deep in her core.

"Slowly, now," Cassandra said. "With all that pent-up energy, we can't have you coming too soon. I want to savor this."

Mia exhaled slowly, drawing her fingers further from her clit, using light strokes and touches that only teased her, nothing more. All the while, she kept her eyes fixed on Cassandra's.

Was she enjoying this? The sight of Mia, her pet, her possession, in the throes of pleasure on her own bed? As usual, her expression gave nothing away. But her eyes were filled with desire, blazing bright as a flame.

Is that because of me? Am I doing that to her?

"Faster," Cassandra commanded, her voice breathy and low. "But don't come yet."

Mia moved her fingers faster, circling and strumming her clit. A moan erupted from her chest, pleasure rising through her.

"That's it," Cassandra whispered. "I want to hear every moan, every cry. Don't hold back."

"Yes, Mistress." Her fingers working frantically between her thighs, she brought her free hand up to her chest, squeezing her breasts, pinching her nipples through her blouse and bra. She shuddered with bliss as her wetness spread on the silk sheets beneath her. *Cassandra's* sheets, on Cassandra's bed, in Cassandra's bedroom.

Everything in this room belonged to her. Including Mia.

Her breaths grew heavy, the ache between her legs deepening. She was so close now. So close!

"Can I come?" she whimpered. "Please, Mistress!"

Cassandra leaned in close, her lips brushing Mia's cheek. "Yes. Come for me."

Mia stroked her fingers faster. Her pleasure rose and rose. And when it finally peaked, her eyes fell shut and her head tipped back, a cry flying from her lips as a climax shook her whole body. Her back arched and her toes curled as she struggled to keep enough control of her fingers to draw out her heavenly release, on and on into infinity.

Finally, she crashed back down to the bed, gasping for breath. But barely a second passed before Cassandra's lips were on hers in a blistering kiss. Mia returned the kiss with lazy lips, too exhausted and weak to move.

When Cassandra allowed her to come up for air, she gathered enough breath to murmur a few words. "I'm sorry."

"What for?" Cassandra asked.

"I closed my eyes."

Cassandra laughed softly. "That's all right." She kissed Mia on the forehead. "You did wonderfully."

"Thank you, Mistress."

Cassandra lay down beside her, wrapping an arm around her. Mia rested her head on Cassandra's shoulder. They lay in silence, Mia basking in the afterglow. She'd never had an orgasm so intense before. And she'd never felt so satisfied.

But she couldn't help wondering how it would feel to be brought to release by Cassandra instead.

A loud ringing crashed through the silence. It was coming from Cassandra's purse on the chair by the bed.

Cassandra pulled away, cursing under her breath. "That's my office ringtone. No one would call me this late at night unless it was important." She got up from the bed. "I'll make it quick."

She pulled her phone from her purse and answered the call. "It's ten o'clock at night. This better be an emergency."

But as the faint crackle of the voice at the other end of the line reached Mia's ears, Cassandra stiffened.

And from her mouth fell a single word, a name.

"*Diane.*"

CHAPTER 16

Cassandra froze in place. She knew that voice. She hadn't heard it in more than a decade, but it was one she'd never forget.

"Well?" Diane said. "Don't you have anything to say to me? It's been so long, after all."

Cassandra's blood turned to ice. Diane was calling her from her own office? How?

Stay calm. This is just one of her mind games. With a glance toward Mia on the bed, she left the room and went into her study, shutting the door firmly behind her.

"I have nothing to say to you," she hissed. "Except that you should be rotting in prison where you belong."

"Now, that's no way to speak to me. After I took you in off the street? After I gave you everything? After I made you the person you are today? I taught you better than that, Cassie."

Just hearing Diane call her that made her skin crawl. "I'm the person I am today because I escaped *you*."

"Oh please. That high-flying career of yours? That fancy penthouse you're sitting in right now? It's all because of me."

Cassandra couldn't deny how much Diane's words rang true. "What do you want?" she spat.

"I want what you took from me. And I'm not talking about the money. Yes, I know you took it. But I don't care about that. Not anymore."

"Then what? What is it you want from me?"

"What do you think? I want my life back! I spent twelve years locked up. I lost everything. All because of *you*. And I know it was you who turned me in. It could have only been you."

"I don't know what you're talking about," Cassandra said.

"Don't lie to me, Cassie. You know what happens when you lie to me."

"Your old tricks don't work on me any longer. I'm not afraid of you."

"You should be. Because you're going to pay for what you did. You took *everything* from me. So I'm going to take everything from you."

"Go ahead and try. You can't hurt me. Not anymore."

Diane scoffed. "You think you're untouchable now that you've made it, don't you? That your status is going to protect you? What was the first lesson I taught you?"

Di's words from long ago rang out in her mind. *Everyone has an Achilles heel. That weak spot, that one thing they care about more than anything. Find it, and you can bring the most powerful of men to their knees.*

"Everyone has a weakness. And you're no exception. So what's yours, Cassie? What is it you care about the most?"

Diane's voice dropped to an almost seductive whisper. "Whatever it is, I'm going to find it. And then, I'm going to rip it from you and burn your life to the ground."

Cassandra spoke through gritted teeth. "Try it. Try it, and I'll make sure you end up right back where you came from. Or worse."

"*Please.* You can posture all you like, but you don't have it in you. I know you better than you know yourself. You never had the spine for anything so distasteful. It's one of my greatest disappointments that I was never able to train that out of you. You had such promise. We could have done wonderful things together. If only you'd trusted me."

"I'd never trust a snake like you."

"Oh, Cassie. We could have taken on the world. Me as queen, you by my side. It's not too late, you know. I'm willing to let bygones be bygones. I'll forgive you for everything, if you'll only come back to me."

Cassandra's grip on her phone tightened. "Even if I believed that... Even if I believed a word coming from your mouth... I would never, *ever* go back to you. Goodbye, Diane. Do not call me again."

Cassandra hung up the call. Her hands were trembling, her body tense with rage and fear. Hearing Diane's voice, hearing her say those things, was more than enough to elicit those feelings in her. But the fact that she'd called Cassandra from her own office? She should have hung up and called the police the moment Diane opened her mouth.

But there was one person she trusted more than the police. Steadying her hands, she dialed Riley's number.

They picked up after a few rings. But Cassandra didn't give them a chance to speak.

"Get security to check my office," she said. "*Now.*"

~

Your office is clear, Riley's message read. *No sign of intruders. No calls logged from any office phones. Nothing on the security cameras. She must have spoofed your number.*

Another message followed, assuring Cassandra that the security teams at her office and apartment building were on high alert. Everything was under control.

So why didn't it feel that way?

She closed her eyes, leaning back in her leather desk chair. Diane hadn't set foot in her office. She'd just wanted Cassandra to think she had. She wanted her to think she'd gotten past all her protections, slipped inside her walls. She wanted Cassandra to feel vulnerable.

But it had all been a ruse. Hadn't it?

Everyone has a weakness. Finding that weakness was Diane's specialty. It was how she manipulated people, extorted them. She'd explained it all to Cassandra back then, explained that for some, their weakness was their family, or a partner, or a loved one. For others, it was their career or their wealth.

But those were only symbols of the things those people truly valued, the intangible things that gave their lives meaning. Reputation. Status. Power. And all of those could be destroyed in an instant.

Where did that leave Cassandra? She had no family to speak of, no loved ones. She didn't care about what people thought of her. Her wealth and possessions? They were meaningless. If she were left penniless, she'd simply start over like she already had before.

That left her career. It was the one thing she'd worked hard to build. The one thing that provided her with a security net big enough for her to never feel powerless again. The one thing she valued the most.

Would Diane figure that out, too?

There was a knock on her study door. "Cassandra?"

She bit back a curse. *Mia.* She'd forgotten all about her.

Cassandra cleared her throat. "Yes?"

"I'm sorry. It's just that you've been in there for a while now. I was worried. I just wanted to make sure everything is okay."

Cassandra got up from her chair and opened the door. "Everything is fine. It was a work emergency. But it's been dealt with."

"Oh. Is there anything I can do to help?"

Cassandra shook her head. "I appreciate your concern, but I'm fine."

Mia had enough on her plate already. The situation with her family, and with the loan shark. No small part of Cassandra wanted to find Bruno herself and deal with the problem once and for all, whether Mia wanted her to or not. Cassandra had friends in high and low places. It would be easy enough.

But that wasn't what Mia wanted. And Cassandra had to respect her wishes, no matter how much it frustrated her.

"Well, I'm here if you need me," Mia said.

She gave Cassandra a soft smile. And for a moment, it was enough to transport her away from all her worldly worries.

An escape. That was what she needed. That was what they both needed.

"You know what?" Cassandra said. "I think we need to get away for a little while. Escape all this stress for a few days."

Was it unwise, given how busy she was with work? Perhaps. But perhaps it would do her good to clear her head.

And it seemed Mia needed a chance to de-stress, too. "You mean, you want to go somewhere?" she asked. "Just the two of us?"

Cassandra nodded. "Just you and me."

Mia's cheeks glowed pink. "I'd like that."

"Perfect. I know just the place. We'll go this weekend. Be sure to pack for cool weather."

Mia nodded. "Yes, Mistress."

"Better still, I'll buy you some appropriate attire. Something for my eyes only, perhaps."

That made Mia blush even more. "I can't wait." She hesitated. "Can I kiss you, Mistress?"

Cassandra nodded. "You may."

Standing on her toes, Mia kissed Cassandra softly on the lips. "Thank you."

"You're welcome. Now go to bed. It's getting late."

Mia left the study, a slight spring in her step. Her excitement was infectious. And there was something satisfying about making her smile.

How much longer could Cassandra keep pretending that Mia was just another submissive? The month was more than half gone now. And with every passing day, their lives became more and more intertwined. Every day, it became harder to deny how deeply she cared for Mia.

Their relationship was just a transaction. It had a time limit. They both knew it. But that didn't mean they couldn't enjoy the time they had left together.

And that didn't mean Cassandra couldn't be everything Mia needed, if only for a weekend.

CHAPTER 17

"We're here," Cassandra said. "Casa de la Diosa."

Mia stepped out of the car. The drive up the mountains had been almost as long as their two-hour flight, first class, of course.

But as she stared up at the mountainside resort, pulling her coat tightly around her to keep out the cool breeze, she couldn't deny that the journey had been worth it. The sprawling chateau stood two stories high, ivy crawling up the stone facade and trailing around stained glass windows. The surrounding mountains were covered in trees, blanketing the ground with red, orange, and yellow leaves.

"This place is amazing," she said.

"You have no idea." Cassandra gave her a knowing smile. "This isn't just any resort. It's special."

Mia didn't get a chance to ask questions before a porter appeared, collecting their luggage and carrying it up to the building. She and Cassandra followed.

"The best part?" Cassandra said. "This is all ours for the next two days."

"Really? We have this whole place to ourselves?"

"Really. The resort belongs to a friend. She let me have it for the weekend as a favor."

They stepped through the front doors and into the entrance hall. The inside was just as grand as the outside. Golden chandeliers hung from vaulted ceilings and antique rugs covered polished hardwood floors. Tapestries hung from the stone walls, vast windows letting in the late afternoon sun and offering a view of the mountains and valleys beyond.

As Mia gazed around in awe, a woman appeared at the top of the grand staircase. She was tall with auburn hair, her scarlet dress the same rich shade as her lipstick.

"Good evening." She descended the stairs gracefully, joining them in the entrance hall. "Welcome to Casa de la Diosa."

"Penelope." Cassandra greeted the woman and introduced her to Mia. "I must admit, I wasn't expecting a personal welcome."

"Given that you're the first guests to stay here, I thought I'd drop in and make sure everything is in place and the staff are prepared. Since this is just a test run, there's only a skeleton staff. A chef, housekeeping, and so on."

"That's very kind of you."

"It's all part of the Casa de la Diosa experience. I'll leave you to discover the rest of what the resort has to offer on your own. But before I go…"

The woman reached into her purse and produced two keycards, one black and one white.

She held up the white card. "This is a key to your room. And this?" She held up the black card, which was inscribed with a gold symbol shaped like an elaborate key. "This is for the other rooms. The rooms with black doors."

She handed both to Cassandra, who took them from her with a nod. Clearly, she knew what the 'other rooms' were.

"I'll leave you to it," she said. "If there are any issues, you have my number. Enjoy your weekend." She glanced at Mia, a gleam in her eye. "I'm sure you'll have plenty of fun."

Mia's cheeks grew hot. What exactly was going on here?

As soon as the woman was gone, Mia turned to Cassandra. "Who was that?"

"Penelope Grant. She's the owner of the resort. And she was polite enough to let us make use of it this weekend in exchange for some feedback on the experience. As I said, this isn't just any resort."

"Right. It's special. But what is it that makes it so special?"

"You'll find out soon enough. Now, why don't we go take a look at our suite?"

Their suite? They were sharing a room? Did that mean sharing a bed, too?

How was she supposed to share a bed with Cassandra, a woman whose very presence sent her heartbeat racing and set her body ablaze? A woman who took pleasure in getting her all worked up, only to leave her aching for more? While she'd finally allowed Mia something of a release, the need she felt for her Mistress had only grown. Every moment they spent together, every time they spoke, or touched, or kissed, Mia only wanted her more. She wanted to be closer to her, to give more of herself to her. She wanted to experience the deepest depths of intimacy with her.

Was it finally time to give Cassandra the very thing she'd 'sold' to her in the first place?

"Is something the matter?" Cassandra asked.

"I…" Mia shook her head. "No."

"Then let's go settle in and relax for a while. Then we'll get ready for dinner."

Cassandra reached out and pushed a stray lock of Mia's hair behind her ear, drawing her thumb down to caress Mia's cheek. "And choose something nice to wear to dinner tonight. Because after? I'm going to show you what makes this place so special."

~

Cassandra set her empty wine glass next to her plate. "That was just delightful. I'll have to pass on my compliments to the chef."

Mia murmured in agreement. Dinner had been incredible. On top of the delicious food, the restaurant boasted an old stone fireplace that filled the room with warmth, and they had their own personal waiter dressed in a crisp white uniform.

Cassandra fixed her eyes on Mia's. "Ready to find out what this resort has to offer?"

"Yes, Mistress," she replied.

But what could the mountainside resort possibly have hidden away that could impress her any more? They'd explored the chateau before dinner, finding a pool room, a theater, a grand ballroom, and more. And that was just on the inside. Outside were tennis courts, a hot tub on the deck, a shed filled with ski gear and other outdoor equipment.

But it was unlikely Cassandra planned for them to spend the evening on outdoor activities. Not after they'd gone to the effort of dressing up for dinner. Just as Cassandra instructed, Mia had dressed in one of the outfits her Mistress had bought for her, an elegant knee-length cocktail dress in a rich, dark purple, accented by a gold necklace and matching bracelet. To finish the look, she'd styled her hair in a loose updo that made it look wavy instead of messy. But she'd left her face bare. While she'd gotten used to wearing the elegant dresses and outfits Cassandra picked out for her—and had even grown to like them—makeup wasn't her style.

And Cassandra seemed more than pleased with the way Mia looked. That much was clear from the way she kept looking at her. Lustful. Possessive. Hungry.

Just like she was looking at her right now.

She rose from her seat. "Follow me."

Heart racing, Mia followed her out of the dining room. They wound their way through the labyrinthine resort, passing a dozen other rooms. And as they traveled deeper into the chateau, Mia noticed that all the rooms around them had black doors.

Finally, Cassandra stopped in front of one of them. "We're here. The resort's premier room. Or so I'm told."

She produced the black and gold keycard, tapping it above the door handle. It unlocked with a click.

But before she opened it, she held her hand out to Mia. "Are you ready?"

Mia glanced at the door. What was inside it? There was only one way to find out.

She took Cassandra's hand. "I'm ready."

Together, they stepped through the door. The room was dark, but only for a moment.

Then, the lights flickered on.

"This is what makes Casa de la Diosa special," Cassandra said. "It has been retrofitted to cater to guests who have... unconventional tastes."

If Mia had ever doubted that described her, she didn't anymore. This room excited her more than anything else in the entire resort.

Yes, it had a bed and all the trappings of a hotel suite. But it was also outfitted with certain other features that couldn't be found in a regular resort room. Arranged on the tables, shelves, and every available surface were a selection of kinky tools and toys, prepped and ready for use. Whips, paddles, riding crops, enough of them to rival the collection Cassandra kept hidden away in her coffee table. Restraints of all kinds, from soft ropes to heavy metal shackles. Dozens of other instruments that Mia didn't even recognize.

And in the center of the room, right in front of the bed, was something Mia *did* recognize. It was a St. Andrew's cross, made of painted black wood, padded and covered with red leather. And attached at the end of each of the arms of the X was a black leather cuff.

Cassandra's eyes fell upon the cross, her lips curling up into a smile. "I can see why Penelope recommended this suite. It certainly delivers." Turning back to Mia, she drew her hand up the side of her shoulder, all the way to her neck. "So now you know why I chose this destination for our little escape. Tonight, I'm going to show you the true meaning of surrender."

Deep in Mia's body, desire sparked to life. Cassandra stepped over to the cross and picked up something hanging from one of the arms, an eye mask made of black leather.

A blindfold.

She turned to Mia, the blindfold dangling from her finger. "Shall we begin?"

CHAPTER 18

Cassandra took Mia's hand and drew her to the center of the room, right in front of the cross.

"True surrender means giving up your power," she said. "Giving up control. And that's why, tonight, I'm going to take both from you, piece by piece."

Mia's pulse began to race. It had been weeks now since she signed that contract, weeks since Cassandra claimed her as her own. She'd spent those weeks in the sweetest agony, waiting, *yearning* for the chance to truly give herself over to her Mistress.

And now, it was finally happening.

Cassandra stepped back. "Take off your dress."

Warmth rose to Mia's skin. Cassandra had already seen her half-naked, but somehow, the idea of undressing in front of her felt naughty. Still, she unzipped her dress, pulled it up over her head, and draped it over a nearby chair, leaving her standing before her Mistress in nothing but her bra and panties.

Cassandra's eyes skimmed her body, her gaze filled with

lust. Mia's breath quickened. She wanted nothing more than for Cassandra to give in to that lust, to drag her over to the bed, throw her onto the mattress, and take the very thing she'd bid for in the first place.

Instead, she held up the blindfold. "Close your eyes."

Mia obeyed. A moment later, the scent of leather flooded her nose as Cassandra slipped the blindfold over her eyes. It was unexpectedly soft and pliable, fitting snugly around her head. She opened her eyes underneath it, but no light reached them at all.

Mia's heart hammered against the inside of her chest. Her Mistress was stripping away her power, just like she'd promised. First her clothes, leaving her naked and vulnerable. Then her vision, leaving her blind, disoriented, wholly reliant on her Mistress to guide her.

She didn't have to guess what came next.

"Turn around," Cassandra said. "Step forward."

Mia walked forward, hands held out in front of her, until they touched the cross. Then, manipulating her like a helpless puppet, Cassandra took Mia's wrists one by one, stretching her arms up and out and cuffing each wrist to an arm of the cross.

"Spread your feet apart," she said.

Mia obeyed. She was still wearing her heels, but Cassandra slipped them off and cuffed her ankles to the bottom of the cross, leaving her strapped to it face first, her legs spread and her ass facing out.

Mia's breath hitched. *Stripped. Blind. And now I can't move.* How much more of her power could her Mistress take away?

"How do you feel?" Cassandra asked. "Comfortable?"

"Y-yes, Mistress." The padding on the cross was firm, the cuffs around her wrists and ankles tight but not constricting. While her body was stretched almost to its limit, she was able to keep her feet flat on the floor.

"Good girl." Cassandra ran her finger down the back of Mia's arm. "Let's begin, shall we?"

Mia's stomach fluttered, excitement and anxiety warring inside her. Cassandra withdrew her hand from Mia's arm, leaving her devoid of any touch, of any sign of her Mistress's presence.

But only for a moment. Because a second later, something brushed against the back of her thigh, a mass of leathery tails sweeping up her skin.

Mia froze. *Is that... a flogger?* Blindfolded, she couldn't see it, but she could feel it.

As the tails of the flogger crept upward, Cassandra's velvet voice rang out behind her. "Remember that night at Lilith's Den? Remember the show we watched?"

Mia nodded. How could she forget?

"Do you know why the woman on stage was so euphoric?"

"N-no, Mistress."

"It's because that surrender? The act of relinquishing control? It brings with it a freedom that cannot be described, only experienced." Cassandra leaned forward, her lips grazing Mia's ear. "I'm going to show you how that feels. I'm going to show you what it's like to have every last sliver of control stripped away."

Mia trembled.

Cassandra stepped back, her heels clicking on the

polished floors. Mia braced herself against the cross, waiting for the flogger to fall—

It hit without warning, a firm slap against the back of her thigh. She sucked in a breath. Just like that morning with the riding crop, Cassandra started slow. But the impact felt greater this time, somehow. Was it because she was blindfolded, her body, her senses on high alert?

Cassandra struck her on the back of the other thigh. Mia jolted against the cross. It was harder this time, but not harder than she could handle. However, Cassandra didn't give her a moment to rest before striking her again, on one ass cheek then the other, over and over in a practiced rhythm.

Mia squeezed her eyes shut tighter under the blindfold. Cassandra wasn't giving her a chance to breathe. She whimpered and writhed against the cross, but that only earned her a firm lash.

She sucked air through her teeth. That one stung.

"Stop moving," Cassandra ordered.

Mia drew in a deep breath and let it out slowly, stilling her body. Her Mistress knew her limits. They'd explored them together. She wouldn't push past them. Mia needed to trust her.

Cassandra brought down the flogger again, raining it upon Mia's ass and thighs with ever-increasing force. But every few strikes, she would stop to gently brush the tails of the flogger over Mia's tender, sensitized skin, or to soothe her aching cheeks with gentle hands. Mia shivered and gasped, overwhelmed by the conflicting sensations.

And slowly, the thrill that came with every strike overshadowed the sting. Slowly, she grew more and more eager for each one.

Slowly, she slipped into a blissful trance.

When the next hit, it sent a quiver through her body from head to toe. A soft moan rose from her chest, her head falling back drunkenly.

"That's it," Cassandra said. "Give in to that feeling."

Mia obeyed. And as she fell deeper into a trance, understanding blossomed in her mind. This was how her Mistress stripped away her power. This was how she stripped away every last sliver of Mia's control. In her intoxicated state, she was helpless to do anything but succumb to Cassandra's will. And with each strike, Mia's soul cried out to her.

I'm yours. I'm yours.

How long did she spend cuffed to the cross while Cassandra flogged her? She'd lost all sense of time, all sense of herself. It wasn't until she felt Cassandra against her, her breasts pressing into her back and her breath on her neck, that she floated back down to her body.

"That's enough," Cassandra said gently. "You've reached your limit, even if it doesn't feel that way."

Mia whimpered in protest. She wanted more. But her whole body ached, nowhere as much as between her legs. And everything she was feeling was starting to overwhelm her.

"Mistress." Her voice trembled as she begged. *"Mistress..."*

Cassandra swept the backs of her fingers down Mia's cheek. "I'm here. I'm right here."

She ran her hands down Mia's body, unfastening the cuffs around her ankles, then her wrists. Freed from her restraints, Mia backed away from the cross, but blindfolded, dizzy and weak with adrenaline and endorphins, she stumbled backward.

Then Cassandra's arms were around her, keeping her steady. "I've got you. I've got you."

She pulled Mia in close, kissing her soft and slow. Mia sighed into her lips, clinging to her desperately. It was enough to ground her, to give her a grip on her surroundings, her senses, her feelings.

And the one feeling that rose above them all was her desire for her Mistress.

Cassandra drew back and took both Mia's hands in hers, leading her forward carefully. Still blindfolded, she couldn't see a thing. But when her legs hit something soft, she realized they were beside the bed.

Cassandra lowered her down to the mattress, then climbed onto it beside her, kissing her again. On her lips. Her chin. Her neck. But no lower. Not where Mia really wanted her.

She let out a pleading whimper. She *needed* her Mistress. She needed her to take what was rightfully hers.

But Cassandra only pressed a finger to Mia's lips. "Not now. Not tonight. You're not in the right state of mind." She traced her finger down the side of Mia's throat. "When I finally take you, you'll be fully present. Fully here with me."

Mia's heart skittered. Not *if*. *When*.

"But I can see how much you need release. So I'm going to allow you to give yourself a little pleasure." She snaked her hands down to the waistband of Mia's panties. "With some help from me."

Slowly, she ran her hands down Mia's sides and peeled her panties from her hips and legs. Then, cupping Mia's hand in her own, she slid it down to where Mia's thighs met.

Mia exhaled slowly. She was so on edge that just the brush of her own fingers was enough to send pleasure shooting through her.

But Cassandra was watching her. And while she'd touched herself with her Mistress watching before, this time, she was blindfolded and even more vulnerable.

"Go on," Cassandra said. "I'll help you."

Releasing Mia's hand, she snaked her own hand back up the center of Mia's stomach, up and over her breasts. Pulling the cups of Mia's bra down, she skimmed her fingers over her nipples, pinching them gently with her fingertips, working them into tight peaks.

Mia inhaled sharply, the throbbing between her thighs too strong to ignore. Parting her legs wide, she slipped her fingers between her lower lips, gliding them over her swollen clit. A tremor rolled through her, pleasure darting deep into her core.

She slid a finger inside herself, then another. A moan spilled from her lips, completely unbidden.

"That's it," Cassandra purred. "I want to hear you sing. I want to feel you come undone."

Her hands still playing at Mia's breasts, Cassandra trailed her lips down her neck, kissing and sucking. Mia arched into her, her fingers quickening between her legs. Blindfolded, in a fog of bliss, it was almost like the fingers between her thighs weren't hers but Cassandra's, stroking and swirling, delving and curling, bringing her closer and closer to the edge.

"Mistress," she cried. "I'm—"

Her orgasm hit her like a crashing wave, flooding her entire body. Her cry was stifled by Cassandra's lips, a fiery, urgent kiss. Mia clung to her, her climax threatening to wash her away, but Cassandra's kiss, the press of her body, was just as unrelenting as the pleasure ripping through her.

It wasn't until Mia's orgasm receded that Cassandra broke away, pulling the blindfold from her head. But Mia didn't open her eyes. She didn't want to come back down to earth. She wanted to linger with her Mistress on this heavenly plane for as long as she could.

Cassandra drew her into her arms once more. "I've got you."

Mia sank into her body, sighing deeply, breathing in the scent of her. She'd never felt so serene, so secure, so *connected* to someone before. And as she finally opened her eyes to gaze upon her Mistress, there was only one thought on her mind.

Was this still just a transaction to Cassandra? Or did she feel what Mia felt?

CHAPTER 19

When Cassandra awoke the next morning, she was alone in bed, the gentle morning sun shining through the windows.

She picked up her phone from the nightstand and glanced at the time. It was already mid-morning. She wasn't one to sleep in, but she and Mia hadn't returned to their suite until late the night before. And even after they got into bed, she'd stayed awake, watching Mia drift off before going to sleep herself.

As she sat up, she heard the door to the suite open, then close again. Moments later, Mia entered the bedroom, a tray laden with food balanced in her hands.

"Good morning, Mistress," she said. "I brought you breakfast."

Cassandra yawned. "You didn't have to. There's room service."

"I know. But I wanted to. Here."

She set the tray down carefully on the bed, the aroma of coffee and freshly baked croissants filling Cassandra's head.

"That smells heavenly." She picked up a cup of coffee and took a sip, a sigh rising from her chest. "This is just what I need. Thank you."

"You're welcome, Mistress."

"Don't just stand there." She reached up and grabbed Mia's hand, pulling her toward her. "Get back into bed and eat this with me."

Mia smiled and slipped back onto the bed, sitting on top of the covers cross-legged. Cassandra moved the tray to rest between them, gesturing for her to eat.

She picked up a croissant and took a bite. "Mm. This is good…" She swallowed. "Seriously, this place is paradise. I'm having the best time. Thank you for bringing me here."

"I'm glad you're enjoying yourself."

Mia blew on her coffee, then sipped it carefully. "You know, this is the first time I've ever been on a trip without my family. Most of the time when we went out of town, it was to take my sister to some specialist. We went on vacations sometimes, but always to places my sister wanted to go, which meant lots of kid stuff. What she wanted always came first. But since we didn't know if she'd even make it to her next birthday, that was understandable."

"I'm sorry."

"It's okay. She's fine now. And now, I'm old enough to go wherever I want, do whatever I want." She nibbled at her croissant. "But I've been thinking about what you said the other day. You know, when I told you about my sister and how my life has always revolved around her. I said that I didn't mind, and it's true. But…"

Cassandra placed a reassuring hand on Mia's knee. "What is it? You can tell me."

"I guess it's just that, sometimes, it bothers me that I never got to have a life of my own. And sometimes… sometimes I even resent her for it." Mia lowered her head, hiding her face. "I've never told anyone that before. It makes me feel so guilty, so *selfish*. Because I just love her so much, and…" She peered up at Cassandra. "Does that make me a bad person?"

"Oh, Mia. Of course it doesn't." Cassandra took her hand. "You've sacrificed so much for the people you love. Given so much of yourself to others. You're allowed to feel the way you do. Feelings are complicated. *Love* is complicated."

"It really is." Mia tucked her legs to one side. "The funny thing is, now that my life doesn't revolve around my family anymore, I don't know what to do with it. Now that I'm free to find my own path, I don't know what path to take. I thought I wanted to go to college, but is that just because it's what you're supposed to do? Is that what I actually want? I've been trying to figure it out, but it's hard, you know?"

"I do. Everyone does. We're all just going through life trying to figure ourselves out. Especially at your age. God knows I felt the same way at 21."

Mia raised an eyebrow. "Really? But you seem so self-assured."

"I wasn't always. After I ran away from home, I spent years and years completely lost. I ended up getting taken in by someone who took advantage of my naivety, but I didn't realize that at the time. It took me years to escape that life. Years to find myself again, figure out who I was in the absence of the person who had defined my existence for my whole adult life. Then I had to work myself to the bone for more than a decade to turn my life around."

"It sounds like you've been through a lot."

"Perhaps. But it left me with a good sense of who I am and what I want out of life, and for that, I'm grateful. It's our struggles that shape us, but it's our choices that show us who we really are. There's no rush to have it all figured out, Mia. Take your time. Explore, live, make mistakes, and pick yourself up to do it all over again. You'll get there."

"I sure hope so." Mia picked up her croissant again and took a small bite. "I suppose I've already figured out a lot about myself lately. Ever since, well…"

"Since what?"

"Since *you*." Mia's cheeks flushed pink. "I've never been in a relationship before. Not even a fling, or something just physical. I've never experienced that kind of intimacy. But I've imagined it. A lot."

Mia's face turned even redder. She glanced down at her half-eaten croissant, avoiding Cassandra's eyes.

"But you've shown me what that's like," she said. "And I know this is just an arrangement, but this whole time, you've made me feel special, and that's something I needed. I never thought I did. I mean, I've never cared about my first time being meaningful. That's why I was willing to sell my virginity in the first place. But being with you has changed that. It's made me realize that I *don't* want my first time to be a night of meaningless sex with a stranger.

"So, I guess, what I'm saying is, I'm glad it was you who won that auction. And I'm glad you didn't just want one night with me. Because I want more than that. I don't need my first time to be with someone I'm in a relationship with.

But I want it to be with someone I trust, someone I feel safe and comfortable with. And in the time we've been together, I've come to feel that way with you."

Mia looked up at her, her eyes filled with desire. No, there was something more there, a current flowing underneath the surface.

"Mistress," she said softly. "Will you—"

But before she could say another word, Cassandra's phone buzzed on the nightstand beside her. And it didn't stop.

She held back a curse. Were the two of them doomed to be interrupted by phone calls at inopportune times forever?

Ignore it. But she'd made it clear to everyone that she'd be out of town this weekend and not to contact her unless it was an emergency.

"Hold that thought," she said.

Pushing aside Mia's visible disappointment, Cassandra reached over to the nightstand and picked up her phone. Riley was calling her. Which meant it couldn't be good news.

She sighed and answered the phone. "What's going on?"

"Sorry to interrupt your trip," Riley said. "Are you somewhere you can talk?"

She glanced at Mia. "Sure. What's going on?"

"There's been a break-in at the Queens Club."

CHAPTER 20

Cassandra stepped out onto the balcony, shutting the door behind her and pulling the robe she'd slipped into tighter around her body to protect herself from the cold morning wind.

"When did this happen?" she asked.

"Last night," Riley replied. "The alarm system was disabled. It wasn't until the morning cleaning crew arrived and saw that it had been disarmed that anyone realized anything was amiss. There were no signs of damage at all. I've had a look myself and I can't find anything. It'll take a little longer to see if anything is missing, or if anything was planted, but there's nothing obvious."

Cassandra cursed. "Are there any cameras nearby? Did you check them?" To protect the privacy of its members, the club itself didn't have cameras, inside or out, but there was a chance a nearby street or traffic camera caught something.

"Already ahead of you. I pulled some strings and got hold of some street cam footage. It showed someone breaking in through a side door around 2 a.m. Couldn't see how they managed to get in and disable the security system, though. And I couldn't see much of the person either. The video was low quality, and their face was obscured."

That wasn't surprising. Anyone clever enough to disable the security system wouldn't be stupid enough to let their face be caught on camera.

But Cassandra didn't need to see the person's face to know who was behind the break-in. *No damage. Nothing taken.* There was only one other reason someone would break into her club.

To send Cassandra a message.

What is it you care about the most? I'm going to find it. And then, I'm going to rip it from you.

How had she been so wrong? It wasn't her company that she cared about the most. It was the Queens Club. It always had been. It was the one thing she held closest to her heart, the one thing she took pride in. A sisterhood, where she'd built not only her professional connections but the personal relationships she'd been missing her entire life. That was what made it precious to her.

She'd never considered that Diane would find out about it. She'd assumed the secret nature of the club was enough to keep it hidden. But Diane had her ways. Uncovering secrets was what she did best.

And now, she knew Cassandra's weakness.

"Cass? Are you still there?"

She steeled herself. "There's been a change of plans. I want security teams to focus on the Queens Club. Leave small teams at my office and apartment building, but I want the majority on site at the club building."

"Understood."

"And remind all security personnel to keep an eye out for Diane."

"I will. So you think Diane did this?" Riley asked.

"I know it. Whether she broke in herself is a different question, but it's irrelevant. Just keep an eye out. And keep searching the building for anything she might have taken. I'll check when the next flight back is. If it comes to it, I can charter a plane."

She glanced at Mia through the balcony doors. She was sitting on the bed inside, oblivious to everything. Could Cassandra bring herself to tell Mia they had to cut their trip short? She'd be so disappointed. But this was an emergency.

"You're coming home?" Riley asked.

"Of course I am."

"I don't think that's a good idea. For all we know, this is a trap Diane is trying to lure you into. It's safest if you stay away."

Cassandra shook her head. "That's out of the question."

"Cass. You said yourself that this woman is dangerous. I'm treating this like a serious threat, and so should you. Stay where you are. I'll scope out the club for you. I know it like the back of my hand. I'll make sure everything is as it should be, sweep the place for bugs. Then when I've confirmed that it's safe, you can come in. Just give me a day or two."

"*Fine.* I'll come back on Sunday evening as planned. But keep me updated. And if anything happens, call me immediately."

"Understood." Riley paused. "Shit. There is something I should mention."

"What is it?"

"When I was looking around to see if anything was out of place, I went up to your office. It was still locked, but I thought I'd check it anyway. And when I went inside, there was something on your desk. I figured you left it there, but it seems out of character. You're not the type for flowers."

"Flowers? What are you talking about?"

"There was a bouquet on your desk."

Cassandra's stomach sank. "What kind of flowers were they?"

"No idea. I don't know anything about flowers. They were a purple-ish blue color. And small. Lots of little flowers on each stem." Riley was silent for a moment. "So you didn't leave them there?"

"No. Diane did, as a message for me." And Cassandra had received it loud and clear. "Thank you, Riley. Call me if you have any updates."

She hung up the phone, dread creeping through her like frost. *A bouquet of small, blue flowers, left on her desk. Belladonna flowers.* A gift from Diane.

A gift, and a warning.

CHAPTER 21

Mia sat on a cushion in front of Cassandra's armchair, right beside her feet, her legs tucked to one side as she watched the fire dance and crackle in the hearth. The staff had lit it for them to warm up the drafty lounge.

She glanced up at Cassandra. She held a glass of wine in her hand, but she'd barely drunk a sip. Instead, she stared at the fire, the flames reflected in her distant gaze.

"Mistress?" Mia asked quietly.

Cassandra glanced down at her. "Yes, Mia?"

"Are you all right? You seem distracted."

Cassandra lowered her hand to Mia's shoulder. "I'm fine. I just have a lot on my plate at the moment."

Did she mean the phone call she'd gotten in the morning? That had to be it. It wasn't the first time.

"Is there anything I can do?" Mia asked.

Cassandra shook her head. "No. And you shouldn't be worrying about me, or anything else. You have no responsibilities this weekend. The whole point of this trip was to escape all that."

"I know. But if you're worried, I can't help but worry, too."

Cassandra gave her a soft smile. "That's sweet of you. But I can take care of myself. No more worrying. That goes for both of us. Let's just enjoy the time we have left. We fly back tomorrow, after all."

Mia sighed. "This weekend feels like it's going by so quickly. This whole month feels like it's flying by."

How much longer did they have left together? 10 days? Fewer? She'd lost count. But they were closer to the end than the beginning.

Did Cassandra feel the same ache at the thought of parting that she did?

Mia had always known exactly what she was getting into. She knew this was just temporary. But from the moment they met, Mia had been drawn to Cassandra.

And now, that attraction had grown into so much more.

She'd told Cassandra as much at breakfast in the morning. At least, she'd tried to. It had all come out jumbled, and they'd been interrupted before she could finish.

But even if they hadn't been interrupted, what would she have said? She barely even understood her own feelings. All she knew was that she wanted Cassandra in a way she never expected to.

"So what do you say?"

"Hm?" Mia shook her head. She'd been staring right at Cassandra, yet she hadn't heard a word she'd said. "Sorry, Mistress."

"That's all right. All I said was let's make the most of our time here. Let's have the perfect night together."

Mia's heart fluttered. "I'd like that."

Cassandra placed her wine glass on the table next to her. "Go up to our suite. You'll find a gift laid out on the bed for you, a new outfit. Get dressed and wait for me in the bedroom."

So Cassandra had something planned for them tonight, too? She wasn't surprised. But something about this felt different from all the other nights, all the other days.

Mia got to her feet and left the room, heading up to their suite. When she reached it, she found an outfit laid out on the bed, just like Cassandra had told her.

But "outfit" barely described it. Because it consisted of nothing more than a short silk robe, a white lace bustier, and a matching thong.

Mia's skin began to burn. She'd been with Cassandra all day. When had she had the time to lay all this out? Or, god forbid, had she asked the housekeeping staff to do it for her?

Mia picked up the thong, dangling it from a finger. It was even skimpier than the lingerie Cassandra had given her to wear to Lilith's Den. And she'd had a dress to wear over it that night. The robe Cassandra had given her would barely cover anything. She'd be practically naked, clad in nothing but scraps of lace.

No, not *scraps*. The lingerie, with its soft, delicate lace, was too luxurious to be called scraps. It was just as she expected from her Mistress. Was it really any different from the expensive dresses Cassandra had her wear every day?

Mia stripped off her dress and her underwear, then slipped into the panties and the bustier, fastening it at the front. It wasn't restrictive or uncomfortable like she expected. It was soft and flexible instead. In fact, she liked the way it hugged her body.

But that wasn't enough to distract her from how awkward she felt in it. This kind of lingerie wasn't for women like her. It was for beautiful women, sexy women, queens and goddesses like her Mistress.

But for whatever reason, her Mistress wanted her to wear it. *If this is what she wants, this is what she'll get.*

She picked up the robe and slid it on, tying it securely around her waist. Then she sat down on the edge of the bed, awaiting her Mistress's arrival.

Not a minute later, she heard the sound of footsteps approaching the bedroom. She rose to her feet just as Cassandra opened the door.

"My, my." Her voice rang out, sultry and smooth, as she stepped into the room. "Look at you."

Mia's pulse raced. There was something in Cassandra's gaze that she'd never seen before. It wasn't hungry, or possessive, or even lustful.

No, it was more like… admiration?

Wordlessly, she beckoned Mia to her. Taking her by the hand, Cassandra guided her over to the full-length mirror in the corner of the room, positioning her in front of it.

"Look." Cassandra took her place behind her, hands on Mia's shoulders. "Look at yourself."

As Mia glanced up at the mirror, Cassandra reached around Mia's waist to untie the belt of her robe, letting it fall open.

"Look," she repeated.

Heart thumping, Mia gazed at the woman before her.

Copper locks cascaded down her shoulders, her hazel eyes piercing, mesmerizing. Her skin was not pale but porcelain. And her curves. They weren't hidden by jeans and T-shirts. They were bared proudly, unashamedly, adorned in silk and lace.

The woman? It was her. This apparition, this beauty, was *her*.

"Do you see?" Cassandra asked.

Mia nodded slowly. She'd never seen herself this way before. She'd never had the chance to. She'd never gotten to be this person, this *woman*. Someone seductive, sensual. Someone confident in herself, her sexuality, her needs. Someone who *desired*.

That woman had never existed outside of Mia's dreams. Until now. Until this moment.

"Now you see it. How captivating you are." Cassandra drew her fingers up the side of Mia's neck. "This is why I tell you what to wear. I want you to feel beautiful. This is why I tell you what to do. I want you to feel desired. And I want you to feel worthy of that desire. Because you deserve it, Mia. You deserve to know how precious you are."

Mia's lips parted in a soft breath. Cassandra's eyes were locked on hers through the mirror, and she could see the desire in them. She could hear it in her words, feel it in her touch. And it only stirred the same within Mia.

From behind her, Cassandra reached up and slid the robe from Mia's shoulders, letting it fall to the floor. Then, she took Mia's chin in her fingers, turning her head toward her, her breath warm on Mia's cheek.

"Mia," she whispered. *"Mine."*

Her lips crashed against Mia's in a tender but unyielding

kiss. Mia exhaled sharply, need rippling through her. Cassandra's hands swept up Mia's sides, caressing her curves through the thin lace, feeling every bare inch of her skin. Mia trembled, her lips growing hungrier, her body pleading for more, *more*.

A desperate whimper fell from her lips. Without breaking the kiss, Cassandra guided her to the bed. Only then did she pull away, drawing her own dress up over her head and dropping it to the floor.

Underneath, she wore a set of matching lingerie made of silk and lace in a shade of crimson so deep it was almost black. But she only gave Mia a moment to admire her in it before reaching behind her back and unfastening her bra, slipping it from her shoulders and freeing her breasts.

Mia stared at her Mistress, clad in nothing but panties and heels. Her long hair was loose and pulled to one side, flowing down her shoulder in a river of silk, and in the dim light of the room, her skin seemed to shimmer.

And her body? If Mia had had any doubts about her attraction to women before, Cassandra's near-naked form was enough to silence them. Every swell and dip, each curve of her hips and breasts, looked like it had been sculpted from the finest marble. Yet at the same time, Mia knew they would feel warm and delightfully soft to touch.

Desire sparked deep within her. Would she get to find out tonight?

Cassandra drew her fingers along Mia's collarbone and down her chest, tracing her fingertips over the cup of the bustier. "I told you to wear this so you could see how beautiful you are. But now, *I* want to see you, all of you." She took a step back. "Show me."

Slowly, Mia undid the clasps at the front of her bustier one by one, then pulled it from her body, dropping it to the floor with Cassandra's dress. Then she reached down and slid her panties down her legs, pushing them aside with her foot.

She was naked now, baring it all for her Mistress to see. And she felt even more empowered than when she'd stood before the mirror with her.

Cassandra's gaze swept up to meet Mia's eyes. "You're even more beautiful than ever."

Mia's breath caught in her chest. She'd never seen such adoration in Cassandra's eyes. And she'd never yearned for her more.

Wordlessly, Cassandra slipped off her heels, pulled Mia onto the bed, and lay on her side next to her, kissing her softly. Mia sighed into the kiss, arching against Cassandra's body. Her hands reached out, caressing her Mistress's soft skin—

Mia pulled back. Cassandra hadn't given her permission to touch her. That was one of her rules, written into the contract that dictated their relationship.

But Cassandra only took Mia's hand in hers. "You can touch me. Just for tonight. Here."

She guided Mia's hand up to her chest, then released it. Tentatively, Mia traced her fingers over Cassandra's breasts, skating her fingertips over pebbled nipples. They were small and pale brown, not unlike Mia's own, but that was where the similarities ended. Cassandra's nipples reacted to the slightest touch, tightening further under Mia's fingers.

A thrill rolled through her. She let her hands wander Cassandra's body, reveling in its novelty. She'd never touched another woman like this before. Cassandra's breasts and hips were fuller than hers, her skin clear and rose-tinted, not pale and dotted with freckles like Mia's. And it was soft, even softer than she'd imagined.

She closed her eyes, immersing herself in Cassandra's body, exploring every inch of her with her fingers. But as she grazed a hand up the inside of Cassandra's thigh, her Mistress took hold of her wrist, pinning it gently to the bed beside her.

"No more." She pushed Mia onto her back. "Tonight is all about *you*."

She pressed her lips to Mia's in a ravenous kiss. Mia rose into her, needing to feel the press of her Mistress's body against hers, skin against skin. She lost herself in Cassandra's lips, her touch, the scent of her, until there was nothing left but *need*.

"Mistress," she whispered. "Please…"

But her words evaporated from her chest as Cassandra kissed her way down her neck and breasts. And when she took a nipple in her mouth, sucking and swirling with her tongue, it sent a jolt of electricity through her that made Mia's whole body quake.

"Oh!" She screwed her eyes shut. "Mistress. *Please.*"

Cassandra peered up at her from under dark eyelashes. "Tell me," she said. "Tell me what you want."

"I want *you*, Mistress."

Cassandra shook her head. "Tell me exactly what you want. *Say it.*"

Mia let out a trembling breath. She knew what her body wanted. But her mind? Her heart?

Did they feel the same?

As she gazed back into Cassandra's eyes, she found the answer in them. "I want you. I want you to make love to me. I want to feel you inside me. I want you to make me yours." Her voice quavered. "Please, Mistress. I want this more than I've ever wanted—"

Her words were cut off by Cassandra's lips, a searing kiss that stole the breath from her lungs and every thought from her mind. Mia wrapped her arms around Cassandra's neck, returning the kiss with famished lips. Cassandra slipped her leg between Mia's thighs, pushing them apart and grinding against her. Mia spread her legs wider, her hips rising from the bed to push back against Cassandra's thigh. She could feel her own wetness on Cassandra's skin, could feel the heat between the other woman's legs.

A moan spilled from Mia's lips. Cassandra slid her hand down Mia's chest, down her stomach, lower and lower, until she reached the peak of Mia's thighs. As she slipped a hand between them, it took all Mia's willpower not to cry out.

"Don't hold back," Cassandra said softly. "Just let go."

Mia closed her eyes, letting her head fall back against the pillows. Cassandra drew her fingers up and down between Mia's lower lips, stroking and circling urgently. Mia quivered and gasped, pleasure rolling through her. And when Cassandra snaked her fingers down to Mia's entrance, the ache of anticipation was almost too much to bear.

"Please," she whispered. "Please…"

Gently, carefully, Cassandra slid a finger inside her. Mia tensed involuntarily. But her Mistress's words echoed in her mind. *Just let go.*

Just let go.

Drawing in a deep breath, she relaxed her body, inviting Cassandra's touch, inviting her in. And after a few moments, she slipped another finger inside her, filling her up.

Mia whimpered feverishly, urging her on. Ever so slowly, Cassandra began to thrust, the heel of her hand rolling over Mia's swollen clit, her fingers curling against that sweet spot inside. And ever so slowly, the pleasure inside her rose and rose like a creeping tide.

Holding tightly onto the back of Cassandra's neck, Mia rocked her hips, tentatively at first, then faster, harder, until they got into a rhythm, moving in time, moving together as one. The room beyond them faded away. The rest of the world faded away. Everything faded away until there was nothing else but the two of them.

And with Cassandra pressed against her, inside her, enveloping her, she reached a crescendo.

"Mistress," she cried. "Cassandra!"

Ecstasy ignited deep in her core, spreading through her like wildfire. She arched up into Cassandra, clutching onto her tightly as wave after wave of pleasure surged through her body. Cassandra held herself against Mia firmly, held herself inside her, riding the storm into oblivion with her.

Finally, Mia's climax faded, leaving a haze of bliss behind. And as she sank into the bed, Cassandra gathered her into her arms, kissing her deeply.

But it was more than just a kiss. More than just an embrace. More than anything Mia could put into words.

Because something had changed between them. Lines had blurred. Boundaries had been crossed. The connection between them had deepened. And what Mia felt toward her Mistress? It had deepened, too.

Her stomach fluttered. And at the back of her mind, a question lingered.

Would she be able to walk away at the end of the month without telling Cassandra how she felt?

CHAPTER 22

"How was the trip?" Riley asked.

"It was fine." Cassandra unlocked the Queens Club doors. They stepped inside. "I needed the break."

She hadn't told Riley about Mia, but a part of her wanted to. A part of her wanted to share that she'd spent an extraordinary weekend with an extraordinary woman, one who she'd slowly come to think of as far more than a hired submissive.

Because that night, in their suite, when Cassandra had finally taken Mia's virginity, offered freely? It had been more than physical. More than just sex.

I want my first time to be with someone I trust, someone I feel safe and comfortable with. And in the time we've been together, I've come to feel that way with you.

Mia had spoken those words to her. And that very night, they had made love for the first time. In that moment, everything between them had felt *real*. In that moment, she'd had everything she'd been searching for—yearning for—within her grasp.

But it was Sunday night now, and she was back home. Back to reality. Back to dealing with Diane and her mission to destroy everything Cassandra held dear.

She marched down the hallway to the elevator, Riley in step with her. "So you haven't found anything else?"

Riley shook their head. "I spent the whole weekend searching this place from top to bottom. There's no sign of damage, no sign that anything was taken or planted, other than the flowers. I even had a specialist team in this afternoon to sweep for bugs and devices. Nothing."

But instead of relief, Cassandra only felt dread. Diane had broken into her club, leaving it completely untouched, just to show her that she could. She still had power over Cassandra. She still had her claws in her. And she'd rather crush her than let her go.

The elevator arrived. They rode it up to the top floor, then made their way to Cassandra's office.

She looked around, examining the room. Everything was exactly as she'd left it. But right in the center of her desk, wrapped in glossy white paper, was the bouquet of little blue flowers.

Cassandra picked it up and tossed it into the trash can beside her desk.

"Are you sure you want to do that?" Riley asked. "It's evidence."

"For who? The police?" Cassandra sat down in the chair behind her desk and leaned back, rubbing her temples with her fingertips. "What would I even tell them? That Diane Whiteford broke into the building to leave me flowers?"

"When you put it that way…" Riley folded their arms across their chest casually. "I should have made the connection as soon as I saw that bouquet on your desk. It wasn't until our phone call that I realized they were belladonna flowers."

"Knowing Diane, that was by design. She loves to play games. Her message was one only I would understand."

"Right. Because you two have some kind of history?"

"You could say that."

Silence fell over the room. But Riley had that look about them, like they had something on their mind, something they were holding back. They didn't like to get involved in anyone else's business. But once they did, they could never keep their opinion to themselves.

Cassandra sighed. "What is it?"

"Well, I did some more digging on Diane," they said. "Just to get a sense of what we're dealing with."

"And?"

"And I found some more information about Belladonna. About how she extracted secrets from people to sell to the highest bidder; that was, if she didn't use it to blackmail or extort them herself. While nothing was ever proven, rumor was that she had a dozen girls working for her. Young women she'd send to seduce her targets. Businessmen, politicians, people in the public eye. They'd form relationships with the men, usually sexual ones, so they could get information from them and relay it back to Belladonna. Or they'd just get evidence they'd slept with the men so she could use that fact against them, threatening to expose their affairs to their families or the public."

Those 'rumors' were true. That was how Diane had operated, pimping out young women to steal their secrets. Of course, Di hadn't seen it that way, and neither had the women. She'd always given them a choice, at least ostensibly.

"Look, Cass. I might be overstepping here, but I'm worried about you."

"If you have something to ask me, just ask," Cassandra said.

"Were you one of Belladonna's girls?"

She shook her head. "No. I wasn't."

"Oh. I just thought—"

"You thought wrong."

No, Cassandra had never been one of those girls. Di had spared her that fate.

But had her own fate been any better? Hadn't she been seduced by the same promises Diane had given to those girls, only to be coerced, manipulated, until she was trapped and powerless, with no way to escape?

Never again. That was the promise she'd made to herself when she left Diane all those years ago. And it was a promise she'd kept. She'd built a life for herself that ensured she'd never be powerless again.

So why did she suddenly *feel* powerless? Why did she suddenly find it so hard to breathe?

"Cass," Riley said. "*Cass.*"

Cassandra shook her head. "Yes. Sorry. I was distracted." And for a moment, the name 'Cass' had sounded uncomfortably close to 'Cassie.'

She drew in a deep, steadying breath. She was not going to let Di get to her.

"Do you want to talk about it?" Riley asked.

"I'd rather not. In fact, I'd rather forget about Diane altogether." She closed her eyes for a moment. "We had a complicated relationship. Although I wasn't one of Di's girls, we were... close."

"I gathered." Riley sat down on the edge of her desk, facing her. "Do you remember when we first met?"

"Of course. Why?" She wasn't exactly in the mood for a trip down memory lane.

But apparently, Riley was. "It was what, six or seven years ago? I'd left the military a few years before, disillusioned by everything I'd seen and done. I figured if I was going to sell my soul, I might as well get paid good money for it. So I went freelance. Took whatever job paid the best. Usually, that meant being a hired gun for wealthy assholes with questionable morals. But within a few years, I'd made enough money to retire and live out the rest of my life doing whatever I wanted, all before I hit 30. But I was still restless. Still unsatisfied."

Couldn't Cassandra relate to that? Having everything—money, success, power—but still feeling like something was missing?

"So when you got in contact, I thought, great, another rich bitch with a messed up job for me to do. But I accepted. I had nothing better to do with myself."

"I had no idea you thought so highly of me," Cassandra muttered.

"That's just it. After that first job, my opinion of you changed." Riley crossed one leg over the other. "I met you in that nondescript coffee shop. You sat down across from me and told me you needed someone for a job. But not just anyone. Someone loyal."

Trust is an illusion. Only loyalty can be bought. That was one of Di's lessons. It had taken Cassandra a long time to shake the woman's influence.

"And you had a look in your eyes that I'll never forget," Riley continued. "This intensity, this determination. But behind it was a weariness. You'd been through hell. You'd lived through things no one should ever have to. And you'd come out the other end, stronger, but not without the kind of scars that can't be seen on the outside. I saw that in your eyes because I saw the same thing when I looked in the mirror."

Cassandra glanced at their face. In all the years they'd known each other, Riley had never spoken of anything so personal. Yet their expression remained as impassive as ever.

"So I was ready for you to offer me some kind of heinous job. Something really fucked up. And I was ready to turn it down, because even I have my limits. But then you told me what the job was. You wanted me to protect a friend of yours. An escort who was in some trouble."

"Kimberly."

Riley nodded. "You told me she'd pissed off the wrong people, and they were after her. You wanted me to play bodyguard for her and her kid while you worked on getting those people off her back. The job seemed like a walk in the park, so I took it.

"But there was one thing I didn't understand. My services don't come cheap. So why would you spend so much money on a bodyguard for some escort and her kid? At first, I thought the two of you were romantically involved. You were an out lesbian, and you wouldn't be the first client to fall for an escort. But that didn't fit."

No, she and Kimberly had never had that kind of relationship. Unlike Cassandra, Kimberly *had* been one of Di's girls, the young women she used to seduce her targets. And she was one of the few Cassandra had had a tentative friendship with. It was why she'd contacted her when Diane got out of prison.

"It wasn't until weeks later when you told me the job was done and you'd personally 'taken care' of the problem that I realized the truth," Riley said. "Kimberly really was just a friend of yours. The two of you weren't even that close. But she was in trouble and you had the power to help her, so you did."

"It was a simple favor," Cassandra said.

But it hadn't been easy to get those men off Kimberly's back. At first, Cassandra had tried to negotiate with them through some underworld contacts she had from her time with Diane. But eventually, she'd simply paid them off, warning them that if they ever went after Kimberly, she'd come down on them, hard. Money talked. So did power. That was another lesson she'd learned from Di.

"Simple or not," Riley said, "what's important is that you didn't have any obligation or responsibility toward her, but you helped her anyway. You, someone who had seen the dark side of humanity, had carried that darkness with you. Yet you still found it in you to help someone, to do some good in the world. I respected that. I still do. Why do you think I've kept on working for you all this time?"

"I… I don't know what to say. Riley, I had no idea you saw me that way."

Riley crossed their arms defensively. "Well, I'm not the sentimental type. My point is, you taught me something valuable back then. Up until that point, all I'd known for half my life was violence. It's what I was trained for, what I was good at. And it made me hate myself and all of humanity. But doing that job for you made me realize I could do some good with my life, that I could rise above everything I'd been through, everything I used to be. I'm stronger than my past. That's what you showed me." They put a firm hand on her shoulder. "And you're stronger than this, Cassandra. Whatever this is? Whatever is going on with Diane? You can beat it. You can beat *her*."

Cassandra shook her head. "It's not that easy."

"I didn't say it would be."

She let out a heavy sigh. "I'm not afraid of her. Not anymore. But if she comes for the Queens Club—"

"I won't let anything happen to the club. My best team is on this place. And I'll be keeping an eye on it personally too. You can count on me."

"I know. And I appreciate it. Thank you, Riley." Steeling herself, Cassandra rose from her seat. "I'm going to take the time to search the club myself. Just in case you missed anything."

Riley nodded. "Good idea. I know this place well, but not as well as you. Call me if you find anything. Or if you just want to talk."

Riley stood up and left the room, their footsteps receding down the hallway. Cassandra took a moment to collect herself, then headed for the door.

As she left her office, she caught a glimpse of the flowers in the trash can. Taunting her. *Warning* her.

Could she ever escape Diane's grasp?

Could she ever truly move on from her?

CHAPTER 23

Cassandra shut her laptop and stretched out in her chair, glancing at the clock on her office wall. *6:28 p.m.* She still had plenty of work to do, especially after taking the weekend and half of Friday off. The sensible thing to do would be to stay in the office for another hour or two to catch up.

Or, she could go home to Mia, who waited eagerly for her to return.

The clock was ticking. In just a week, their arrangement would end. Their contract fulfilled, they would go their separate ways.

And Mia would be gone from her life forever.

Could Cassandra simply accept that? A part of her wanted to cast aside all her doubts and tell Mia how she felt. But the rest of her? It still felt the pain of the last time she'd fallen in love. She remembered how it had left her shattered. She remembered how long it had taken her to pick up the pieces and forge them into something stronger.

But the cracks were still there, vulnerable, weak. And parts of her were still missing, or broken beyond repair.

Her phone vibrated, a reminder flashing on her screen. *Dinner with Ava and Tess at 7:30.*

She cursed. She'd arranged to catch up with the couple once they got back from their vacation, but with how hectic the past few weeks had been, it had completely slipped her mind.

Cassandra picked up her phone and dialed Mia's number. She needed to tell her that she wouldn't be home until late. A text message would have been quicker, but a part of her simply wanted to hear Mia's voice after a long day.

Had she ever felt that way about a woman before?

Mia answered the call, greeting her warmly.

"Mia, I'm sorry for the late notice," Cassandra said, "but I have dinner plans tonight. I won't be home for a few more hours."

"Oh. Okay. Thank you for letting me know."

Cassandra felt a pang of regret. Mia's disappointment was clear in her voice. Did she feel it too? The specter of time hanging over them?

"You know what?" Cassandra said. "Why don't you come with me? Be my dinner date?"

For a moment, there was only silence at the other end of the line.

And for a moment Cassandra was left wondering why she'd said such a thing to Mia in the first place.

"If you'd rather not—"

"No," Mia interjected. "I mean, yes. Yes. I'd like to come to dinner with you."

"All right. I'll text you the address and meet you there."

She hung up the phone and sent the address of the restaurant to Mia, then began packing up her desk to leave.

Cassandra sat beside Mia, sipping on a vodka martini while they waited for the others to arrive. Mia had ordered an elaborate cocktail in an enormous glass. Already, she'd almost finished it.

She sucked up the last of the drink through her straw. "I can't wait to meet these friends of yours. I'm really curious about them. And I was beginning to wonder if you had any friends."

"Oh?" Cassandra crossed her arms. "And what does *that* mean?"

A red flush crept up Mia's face. "I don't mean that in a bad way! It's more that you seem like the kind of person who doesn't need anyone else. But I like that about you." She gave Cassandra a playful smile. "This whole strong and independent thing is kind of sexy."

Cassandra eyed Mia's glass. "How much alcohol was in that thing?"

"I'm not drunk. Well, maybe I shouldn't have had this on an empty stomach. But I mostly just feel… happy." She stirred the remaining ice in her glass around, her eyes growing distant. "It's funny. With everything that's going on, with Bruno breathing down my neck and my family's, I should be worried. I should be scared. But I'm not. I feel like I don't have a care in the world. I feel free. And I don't think I've ever felt this way. Not before I met you."

Something tugged in Cassandra's chest. How easy it would be to take Mia's hand and tell her she felt the same way. How easy it would be to tear up their contract and ask Mia to stay for another week, another month, another year.

How easy it would be to ask Mia to be hers, not for money but so they could explore what they shared more deeply, see where it would lead them.

But before either of them could say a word, a pair of women appeared at their table. One was taller and around Cassandra's age, while the other was younger, with light brown hair and a bubbly smile.

Cassandra rose to her feet, embracing them both. "It's so good to see you." She gestured toward Mia. "Let me introduce you. Mia, meet my good friend Ava. And this is her fiancée, Tess. They got engaged recently."

Mia stood up. "Nice to meet you. And congratulations."

With greetings and introductions done, all four of them took their seats.

"How was your anniversary trip?" Cassandra asked. "Spain, wasn't it?"

"It was incredible," Tess, the younger woman, said. "We stayed at the most beautiful villa and ate the most amazing food. And the beach, and the landscapes—it was like something from a postcard."

The conversation continued, only stopping to allow the server to take their orders. Ava had been just as busy as Cassandra of late, so it had been an age since they'd gotten the chance to catch up. Cassandra hadn't told her anything about Mia beyond promising to explain everything when they had a private moment. And while Ava didn't pry, her curiosity was clear on her face.

As Tess and Ava told them all about their wedding plans, the conversation inevitably turned toward their relationship, with a polite question from Mia about how they met descending into a lengthy retelling of their tumultuous history together. It wasn't until they were halfway through the main course—and on to their second bottle of wine—that Ava announced she'd asked Cassandra to dinner for a reason.

"Do you need a favor?" Cassandra said. "I'm always happy to help out."

"It's always business with you, isn't it? But you're right. I do need a favor." Ava looked at her fiancée. "And it's a big one."

Cassandra glanced between the two women. "What is it?"

"Cassandra Lee," Ava said. "Will you be my maid of honor?"

It took her a moment to process Ava's words. "You want *me* to be your maid of honor?" While the two of them were close and had been friends since business school, Cassandra was hardly the romantic type. Weddings were *not* her domain.

"Of course. Cass, you're my dearest friend. You've done so much for me *and* Tess. I want you with me every step of the way. So, what do you say? Because my backup is Riley, and it would be cruel to subject them to hours of wedding dress shopping."

Cassandra nodded. "Yes. Of course I will."

Ava smiled. "Wonderful. It's still a year away, but we want to start preparing now. We're having it on the island,

and the guest list will be small, but there's still so much to do."

"Seriously," Tess said. "I had no idea how much work was involved in a wedding. It's not just cakes and flowers. We even have to pick what kind of napkins we want."

Ava put her hand on Tess's arm. "Like I told you, we can leave all that to the planner."

"I know, but where's the fun in that?" Tess teased.

A smile pulled at Cassandra's lips. She'd never thought of Ava as the type to ever get married, but she'd found the perfect match in Tess.

The perfect match. That was something Cassandra had never wanted. She didn't want *perfect*. She wanted *real*. And what was more real than this? Sharing a meal with her oldest friend, Mia by her side?

It felt real. It felt *right*.

She turned her gaze to Mia, who nodded along, stars in her eyes, as Tess told her all the intricate details of their private island wedding. Was Mia dreaming of the same thing? Of falling wildly in love, of getting engaged, of standing before the altar, pledging her heart to another for the rest of their lives?

Was it Cassandra she saw in her mind when she imagined it?

Cassandra shook her head. She was on her second glass of wine, and she'd already had a drink before dinner. Clearly, it was going to her head.

She stood up and placed a hand on Mia's shoulder. "Excuse me for a moment."

Cassandra made her way to the restaurant bathroom. There were only two stalls, one occupied, one out of order.

She splashed some water on her face as she waited, but it did little to clear her head.

Because she wasn't drunk in the first place. All the thoughts of Mia swirling around in her head? She couldn't blame them on a loss of inhibitions. The feelings, the desires, the longing for something more?

All were more real than anything she'd ever felt.

Behind her, the stall door opened. As Cassandra turned, a woman strode out of it. An older woman with pale skin, dark hair streaked with white, and the most disarming smile Cassandra had ever seen. A woman who had haunted her for more than a decade.

Diane.

Cassandra's heart stopped. Twelve years. It had been twelve years since she'd seen the woman's face outside of her nightmares.

This wasn't a nightmare. Di was here, in the flesh.

"Hello, Cassie," she said.

"Diane." Cassandra kept her voice steady and firm. She wasn't going to let the woman know how rattled she was by her presence.

"That's no way to greet me." She stepped toward Cassandra until barely a foot separated them. "Didn't I teach you better than that?"

"Considering you've spent weeks stalking and threatening me, manners are the least of my concerns right now."

"Threatening you? You think I was..." Diane laughed. "If you're talking about the flowers, that was a peace offering. After I called you, I realized I might have come on a bit too strong, so I thought I'd extend an olive branch. That's why I'm here. I just want to talk, see if we can work things out."

Cassandra shook her head. "You're insane. I'm done talking with you. I want *nothing* to do with you."

"How can you say that? After all we went through together? After everything we shared?"

Cassandra scoffed. "Everything we shared? Don't pretend we were ever partners. Don't pretend you weren't just using me the whole time. I was a tool to you, just like everyone else."

"You're wrong. Cassie, I loved you."

"You didn't love me. You're incapable of love. You're incapable of feeling anything at all."

Diane clutched a hand to her chest. "Is that really how you see me? As some kind of monster?"

"That's what you were, Di. What you *are*. But there's no use trying to make you see that. No use trying to reason with you. It took me far too long to realize that. Far too long to leave. But I did. I moved on. And I will not be dragged back into your games!" Cassandra lowered her voice. "So leave me alone to live my life in peace."

Diane's lips curled into a sneer. "Ah, yes. Your picture-perfect life. You have it all, don't you? A successful career. More money than you could ever spend. And now, a pretty little thing by your side."

Dread washed over her. *Mia.* Did she know about Mia?

"I was very surprised to see you here with someone tonight," Diane said. "Who is she? Should I be jealous?"

So she didn't know who Mia was. And Cassandra intended to keep it that way.

"She's no one. Just an escort I hired." It was close enough to the truth that if Diane looked into it, she'd find nothing to say otherwise.

"Developed a taste for young women, have you? You're not so different from me."

Anger rose in Cassandra's gut. "I am *nothing* like you."

"Oh please. You and I are alike in every way. Why do you think I chose you in the first place? I saw your potential. And now you're finally living up to it, all thanks to me. Don't try to deny it. I taught you everything you know. The art of negotiation, manipulation. How to influence others, gain their trust. How to use their hopes, their fears, to your advantage. You took those lessons and used them to climb the corporate ladder, to build your empire. And to create your precious Queens Club."

Cassandra grimaced. It was true. So much of what she'd learned from Diane had been useful in building her career. But she'd never resorted to dirty tricks like Diane had. She'd never manipulated anyone, used anyone.

"Lie to yourself all you want," Diane said. "But we both know the truth. I *made* you, Cassie. I trained you, molded you to be my right-hand woman. I gave you everything. And then you betrayed me."

Diane's eyes narrowed into slits. Her smile was gone now. And in its place was cold, hard fury.

"I'm sorry," Cassandra said. "I'm sorry for my part in what happened to you. And I'm sorry for taking your money. I'll pay it all back—"

"I don't want your money! I want you to suffer like I have!" Diane leaned forward, spittle flying from her lips as she hissed into Cassandra's ear. "You were precious to me. Then you betrayed me. So I'm going to take away what's most precious to you. I'm going to make you *hurt*."

Cassandra tensed. Di had turned on her on a dime. Just

like she did back then. And just like back then, Cassandra was paralyzed.

Pull yourself together. She wasn't the girl she'd once been. She wouldn't be bullied by Diane. She wouldn't be controlled by her.

But before she could say another word, the bathroom door swung open. In walked another customer, barely glancing in their direction as she made a beeline for the open stall, shutting the door behind her.

Diane stepped back. "This isn't over, Cassie. Next time we meet, I won't be so nice."

She turned and left the bathroom, the door swinging shut behind her.

Cassandra let out a breath. She'd been gripping the counter behind her so hard that her fingers were numb. She shoved down the panic in her gut, but she couldn't stop it from rising back up.

I need to get out of here.

Erecting a stone facade, she left the bathroom and marched back to the table. "I'm sorry, but something has come up. We'll have to cut dinner short." She put a hand on Mia's arm. "We need to leave."

Mia frowned, but didn't question her. She set her napkin down next to her nearly empty plate and got to her feet.

"Is everything all right?" Ava asked.

"Everything is fine." While Cassandra had told her about Diane in vague terms, she didn't have time to get into the details now, nor did she want to. "I apologize for leaving you in the lurch like this. I'll call you so we can reschedule for another time."

Taking Mia's hand, she said a polite goodbye and pulled her toward the restaurant's exit.

As they waited outside for her driver to pull around, Cassandra scanned the street for any signs of Diane. But what did it matter if the woman was lurking nearby? Diane had already proven how easily she could get to her. It was only a matter of time—

"Cassandra. *Cassandra.*" Mia wrenched herself from her grasp. "What's going on?"

"It's nothing." Their car pulled up in front of them. "Get in."

Cassandra opened the door and ushered Mia into the back seat, sliding in behind her. As the car took off, Mia battered her with questions until Cassandra gave her a look that silenced her completely.

She didn't miss the hurt expression on Mia's face. But she had other things on her mind. Diane was becoming more and more unhinged. More and more brazen. She was intent on destroying Cassandra.

And she wouldn't rest until she had.

CHAPTER 24

Are you coming to the play? Mom wants to know so she can buy tickets.

Mia took a seat on the couch, curling her legs up underneath her as she sent Holly a reply. *Of course. How could I miss my sister's big debut?*

Mia could practically see the eye roll that accompanied her sister's next message. *You're almost as bad as Mom. I only have a supporting role, but she's acting like I'm the star.*

Mia smiled. That was just like her. *How's Mom doing, anyway?*

Fine, I guess. Busy with work, but that's nothing new. Why?

No reason. Just checking up on things.

After their conversation about Bruno, her mom had promised to let Mia know if he returned or if she noticed anything suspicious. So far, her mother had told her, nothing was amiss. But Mia could hear the anxiety in her voice every time they spoke.

Soon. Soon, I'll be able to pay him everything I owe. Soon, it will all be over.

Soon, I'll say goodbye to Cassandra forever.

Mia glanced in her direction. Cassandra was seated at the other end of the couch, typing away at her laptop. She'd come home from work an hour ago, then promptly sat down with her laptop, muttering about all the work she had to do for a recent acquisition, barely giving Mia so much as a glance.

But was Cassandra's distant manner really because of work? It had all started after dinner on Monday night. The dinner she'd spontaneously invited Mia to, where she'd introduced her to her closest friends. The dinner that felt so much like a date that Mia had started to wonder if it really was one.

The dinner Cassandra had ended prematurely, dragging Mia out of the restaurant. And she'd been cold and guarded ever since.

What had happened that night?

"Cassandra?" When she didn't respond, Mia tried again. "Mistress?"

"Yes?" she murmured.

"Is everything okay? You seem tense, that's all."

Cassandra continued to type, her eyes not leaving her screen. "Like I said, I have lots of work to do."

"Right."

Was she lying? Or was Mia reading too much into things? Maybe it really *was* just work that had Cassandra preoccupied. That was nothing new. The two of them had been interrupted by Cassandra's work calls and emergencies all month.

And even if there was something else going on, why

would Cassandra tell her about it? After all, Mia was just someone she was paying to serve her.

She sighed. Just when she'd started to feel like there was something between them, Cassandra had shut her out. Now, Mia didn't know where she stood.

"I can't concentrate with you sighing like that," Cassandra murmured.

"Sorry." Mia uncurled her legs from underneath her and stood up. "I'll just go to my room."

"No. Mia, wait."

Cassandra shut her laptop, setting it aside on the coffee table and grabbing hold of Mia's hand to pull her back down to the couch.

"You're right," she said. "I've been preoccupied. I've been brushing you off, and I'm sorry. I just have a lot going on right now."

"You mean, with work?"

"Among other things."

Mia hesitated. "Do you want to talk about it?"

Cassandra shook her head. "I'd rather not. I'd rather not think about it at all." She leaned forward, a hand on Mia's knee. "In fact, I'd rather take my mind off it completely."

Cassandra snaked her fingers up the front of Mia's thigh, sending a spark through her. That night they shared in the mountain chateau had been perfect. But it had done nothing to quench her desire for Cassandra. If anything, it had made Mia want her more. Every inch of her body craved her Mistress.

But her mind? It was elsewhere. It was picturing the way Cassandra had dragged her out of the restaurant. It was trying to figure out why she'd turned from hot to cold in the blink of an eye. It was still trying to puzzle through all the conflicting feelings she had about what was supposed to be just an arrangement, but felt like so much more—

And when Cassandra's lips collided with hers, it awakened a yearning in her that was stronger than everything else she felt.

Mia murmured into the kiss, her hands grabbing at the front of Cassandra's blouse to steady herself. In response, Cassandra ran her hands up Mia's chest, pushing her down to the couch.

A gasp rose from her lips. Cassandra smothered it with a kiss that sent need shooting straight into her core. *Devour me*, she whispered in her mind. *Make me yours.*

But Mia wasn't really hers. And she never would be. Not when their relationship had an end date. She wanted so badly to tell her Mistress how she felt. But how could she, with Cassandra acting the way she was?

Was it stupid of her to consider confessing her feelings in the first place? From the very beginning, Cassandra told her that she wanted a submissive, not a lover. And certainly not a relationship.

So why did she kiss Mia like she did?

Without warning, Cassandra's hands were around Mia's wrists, pinning them to the couch on either side of her.

"You know the rules," she said. "No touching me without my permission."

Mia had been so lost in her head that she hadn't noticed what her hands were doing. "I'm sorry."

"Sorry, who?"

"I'm sorry, *Mistress*."

"Much better."

Mia's stomach fluttered as Cassandra kissed her again. But her hands were still clamped around Mia's wrists, the full weight of her body on top of her. It was no different from the night they made love. No more intense than being tied up in ropes, or cuffed to a cross and blindfolded.

But this felt different. This felt *wrong*. Mia didn't want this. She didn't want to be Cassandra's servant, a toy for her to use and throw away. Because that was what was going to happen to her at the end of the month.

Something tightened in Mia's chest. Why was it suddenly so hard to breathe?

She shifted under Cassandra's body, breaking off the kiss. "Cassandra, stop." Her voice quivered as she spoke. "Tiger. Tiger!"

At once, Cassandra let go of her wrists, pulling away and getting to her feet. Mia sat up, her whole body shaking.

"Are you all right?" Cassandra asked. "What's the matter?"

"I'm fine. I just…" Mia wrapped her arms around herself. "I don't want to do this."

Cassandra nodded. "Okay. That's all right. You did well speaking up. We don't have to do this. We don't have to do anything you don't want to. That was always the agreement."

An agreement. That was all this was. A contract. A transaction.

Mia shook her head. "You don't understand. I don't want to do this. I don't want to do any of this. I'm not a toy. I'm not a thing for you to use and throw away when you're done with me. I'm a person! I have feelings!"

"Of course. And I know that."

"Then why? Why do you keep treating me like I'm just your doll? Why can't you see that I—"

A tremor rocked Mia's body. She swallowed a sob, hot tears welling in her eyes. She couldn't break down in front of Cassandra. Not when she didn't even understand why she was breaking down in the first place.

Cassandra placed a hand on her arm. "Mia—"

But Mia shook her off. "I'm going to my room."

Ignoring Cassandra's protests, she got up and fled to her room, locking the door behind her. Then she sank to the floor, her back against the door, her knees pulled up to her chest.

Only then did she let her tears fall. And once they started, she couldn't stop them. She couldn't hold back her feelings.

She'd fallen for Cassandra. And she had to tell her before it was too late.

CHAPTER 25

Cassandra sat in the darkness of the living room, Mia's words echoing in her mind.

Cassandra, stop.

How long had passed now, since Mia locked herself in her room? Minutes? Hours?

I don't want to do this. I don't want to do any of this.

How could she have been so blind? How could she not see that she'd pushed Mia too far?

How could she not see that Mia was hurting?

I'm not a toy. I'm not a thing for you to use...

She'd been so wrapped up in her problems that she hadn't noticed anything was wrong. If she'd been paying attention, doing her job as Mia's Domme, she would have seen it. But she'd been treating Mia like a doll, using her to soothe her own feelings, just like Mia had said.

Cassandra shook her head. She'd told herself that by bidding on Mia, she was trying to save her from being used by callous monsters who had no regard for her feelings. Yet here she was, doing exactly that to Mia.

Doing exactly what had been done to her.

Or maybe she'd been lying to herself all along. Hadn't she been taking advantage of Mia from the very beginning? She was holding two million dollars over her head, holding her hostage for a whole month. Mia had never had a choice but to do whatever Cassandra wanted her to do. Had she ever really been a willing participant?

No, Mia had been willing. Eager, even. Just like Cassandra had once been.

And that only made it worse. Mia was a submissive through and through. She'd wanted this. She'd wanted to serve Cassandra, learn from her. She'd put her trust in Cassandra, giving herself over to her. And somewhere along the way, Mia had developed feelings for her, *real* feelings.

Cassandra had seen it. She'd tried not to. Because that would have forced her to face her feelings for Mia, too.

But it didn't matter how either of them felt. Because in the end, Cassandra had become the very monster she'd been trying to save Mia from. She'd become her worst nightmare.

She'd become Diane.

Cassandra buried her face in her hands. She was too broken, her heart too damaged. She couldn't give Mia what she needed. Couldn't be what Mia needed her to be. Her Domme. Her lover. Her partner.

Because the depth of surrender that required, both from Mia and from Cassandra herself? That true, unwavering surrender she'd been seeking for half a lifetime? It couldn't exist without love. And she could never love Mia the way Mia needed her to.

Cassandra had to end things before she hurt Mia more.

Cassandra barely slept that night. But when she finally woke up after drifting off in the early hours of the morning, the first thing she did was call in to the office and clear her schedule for the morning.

She had something more important to take care of.

As she sat in the living room, finishing off her morning coffee, Mia emerged from her bedroom, freshly showered and dressed. She didn't usually wake up so early. Had she lain awake in bed all night too, unable to sleep, racked with worry? Had it been a mistake on Cassandra's part to give her space instead of comforting her?

But that would have only given Mia hope for something that could never be. Cassandra needed to get this over with as quickly as possible. It was kinder that way.

She set down her coffee as Mia approached.

"Um, can we talk?" Mia asked.

Cassandra nodded. "I have some things I need to say, too. Why don't you sit down?"

Mia took a seat at the other end of the couch, wringing her hands in her lap. "I want to apologize for last night."

"You don't need to. You did nothing wrong."

"No, I do. All those things I said, I didn't mean them. I was just feeling emotional, and suddenly, it was all too much. I said those things because I was upset, not because they're how I really feel."

"It's me who should be apologizing. I should have noticed you weren't in the right headspace and stopped before things got that far. I'm sorry, Mia. It's no excuse, but I've been dealing with some problems of my own. They've left me unable to give you the attention you need. That's why I need to end our arrangement. That's why I never should have started it in the first place."

All color faded from Mia's face. "You want to end things?"

"You'll still get the money. I'll make sure of it. I'm a woman of my word."

Mia shook her head. "It's not the money. I just... I don't understand. What's going on?"

There was no reason to tell Mia about Diane. And even if Cassandra wanted to tell her, how could she explain it all? How could she explain the scars Diane had left on her?

But didn't Mia deserve to know why she had to end things between them? As much as she tried to deny it, the two of them had a connection. They'd grown to care for each other deeply. Leaving Mia in the dark, wondering why she'd been cast aside, would be cruel.

After all they'd been through together. After all Cassandra had put her through. Didn't she owe Mia the truth?

Cassandra folded her hands in her lap. "Do you know why I bid on your auction, Mia?"

Mia shook her head. "You said it was just a whim."

"That's true. But there's more to it than that. When I saw you on that website, all I could see was myself years ago. Young. Naive. Desperate. Completely unaware that I was in way over my head. And when we met in person, it only confirmed my assumptions. You're a submissive in your soul. You want to give yourself to someone completely. That, combined with your naivety, was dangerous.

"You were a magnet for the wrong kind of person. The

kind who would place value on a submissive woman's virginity and pay millions for the chance to take it in whatever cruel way they desired. That's why I needed to win your auction. I wanted to save you from that fate, Mia. I wanted to save you from a fate like my own."

"What... what happened to you?" Mia asked.

"Where do I even begin?" Cassandra sat back in her seat. "I suppose it all started when I ran away from home. I'd spent my entire childhood clashing with my strict, religious parents. It only got worse as I got older. And when I was 17, my parents caught me in my bed with a friend, another girl, doing things that were decidedly not platonic."

Cassandra didn't know what had enraged her parents more. The discovery that their daughter was a lesbian, or the fact that she was having sex. Because to them, both were the most terrible of sins.

"After that, my parents went from strict to abusive," she said. "I had no one to turn to. No one I could go to for help. So I decided to run away, because nothing could be worse than staying. I caught a bus across the country with a backpack full of clothes and all the money I'd saved from my summer job. But the money didn't last. And I ended up on the streets."

It had been a difficult period in Cassandra's life. But it hadn't been the *most* difficult. That had come after.

"While I won't go into detail," she continued, "my situation became desperate. Desperate enough for me to consider doing things I never thought myself capable of, just to survive. I had no other options. I'd turned 18 by then, so even if I'd wanted to return home, my parents had no obligation to take me in. I had nowhere to go. Then, I met Diane."

Mia's brows drew together. Had she overheard Cassandra talking about Diane before? But if she recognized the name, she didn't say anything.

"Di ran a number of homeless shelters around the city. She was something of a philanthropist, pouring her free time and money into charitable pursuits. That was how we met. I stopped by one of her shelters for a meal, and she introduced herself to me. And whenever I returned, she'd take the time to talk to me. Slowly, I began opening up to her. Slowly, I began to trust her."

In hindsight, Diane had been manipulating her from the very beginning. But at the time, Cassandra had been so starved for any human connection that she'd been blind to the warning signs.

"So when Di offered to take me in, I jumped at the chance," Cassandra said. "She told me she sometimes took girls in to help them get back on their feet, and she wanted to do the same for me. She said that I had too much potential to waste my life on the streets. She made good on her promise, sheltering me in her own home, giving me food, clothing, everything I needed. And gradually, we became... close. Emotionally. *Physically.*"

Understanding dawned on Mia's face. Cassandra pushed down the shame rising inside her. "Looking back, it was all by design. Di, she showered me with gifts, with compliments, telling me how special I was. My whole life, I'd never been shown that kind of love. So I fell for it hook, line, and sinker. But what really made me fall for her? What really got me under her spell? It was when she introduced me to a world I knew nothing about, one I became completely enamored with. And from then on, she wasn't just my girlfriend, my lover. She became so much more than that."

Cassandra looked into Mia's eyes. She was hanging on Cassandra's every word.

"Diane," she said. "She became my Domme."

CHAPTER 26

"She was your Domme..." Mia echoed, hardly comprehending her own words. "So, you were her submissive?"

Cassandra nodded. "It was what I wanted at the time. And it felt natural to me. I was attracted to Diane's strength, her power. And I was drawn to the feelings of safety and security that kind of relationship provided. It made me happy. At least, for a while."

While Cassandra's words were bittersweet, all Mia could hear in her voice was bitterness, the pain in her eyes breaking through her stoic facade.

"But it was only a matter of time before she showed her true colors," Cassandra said. "And in more ways than one. One night, she said she wanted to tell me the truth about who she was, what she did. Her philanthropy was just a cover for her real profession. She was an information broker. She obtained secrets and confidential information on people and organizations, trading it, selling it, using it to further her interests.

"And getting that information? That was where the young women she helped came in. They were runaways, people living on the margins of society. She'd take them in and give them new lives, training them to do her bidding. Then she'd send them out to seduce her targets, gaining their trust and getting them to spill their secrets. Or she'd simply have the women sleep with them so she could blackmail them."

Bile rose in Mia's stomach. "So, she was some kind of pimp?"

"In a roundabout way, yes. But she didn't see it that way. And neither did her girls. They served her willingly. After all, she always took good care of them, made sure they had everything they needed. And she always gave them a choice. But is it really a choice when the alternative is being out on the streets? When your Mistress is someone as powerful as Di? Someone as vengeful?"

Cassandra's hands curled into fists in her lap, her knuckles white. Was she still talking about those *other* girls?

"She framed herself as some kind of Robin Hood," she continued, "mostly targeting bad men, corrupt ones. But everything she did was for personal gain. And she was in business with criminals, and worse. That was how she gained her nickname. *Belladonna.* She was notorious in the underworld. No one knew who she was or how she gained her information. No one knew about her girls.

"And the night she told me all this? She also told me *I* was supposed to be one of those girls. That was why she'd taken me in in the first place. But then she'd realized I was different, she said. She saw something of herself in me, in how smart and ambitious I was. I'd always been that way, even as a child, but I was never good enough for my parents. They crushed any sense of self-worth I had."

Mia felt a pang of sympathy. It was no wonder Cassandra never wanted to talk about her family.

"But Di? She said I was special. I was meant for great things, just like her. And she wanted me by her side." Cassandra shook her head. "At least, that was what she would tell me. In truth, she simply wanted to *own* me, keep me locked up in her house with all her other possessions. That's what I was to her. A doll she could bend and shape to her will. I became something of her protege, too. She taught me all about her business, grooming me to be a part of it. And I was so in love with her that I was willing to go along with it all, despite knowing what she was doing was wrong. Despite knowing she had a dark side. And over time, that side of her spilled into our relationship."

Cassandra's eyes grew distant, but her body was tense, like she was fighting off memories. But Mia didn't interrupt. Not when her Mistress was pouring her heart out to her.

Cassandra's voice wavered as she spoke. "She became controlling, dictating every element of my existence, whether I wanted her to or not. And she had a temper. She'd punish me if I disobeyed her or displeased her in any way. And I put up with it because she was my Mistress. She *owned* me. At the time, I didn't know that wasn't how those kinds of relationships are supposed to work. I didn't know any better. We never had any discussion about limits and boundaries, about what we were both comfortable with. I just had to do what she wanted, when she wanted it. I had a safe word, but she would get angry at me if I used it, so it was easier to just keep quiet and push through whatever she wanted to do to me."

A knot formed in Mia's chest. How could she express her horror, her anger, at how Diane had treated her? What could she say to her that wouldn't sound inadequate? There were no words for something like this.

Cassandra shook her head. "I shouldn't have put up with it. But I was so blinded by everything she did for me, by my feelings toward her. I know now that what I felt for her was out of desperation and dependence rather than love. Her home was my home. She was all I had. I couldn't even comprehend the thought of leaving her. So I stayed. For five long years, I stayed. During that time, I tried to leave her, more than once. But I'd always get pulled back in. And then things would get better. And then things would get worse and worse."

Cassandra's balled-up fists trembled in her lap. Mia longed to comfort her, with a word, a touch. But that wasn't what she needed right now. She needed to get everything out.

"Eventually, things got so bad that I knew I had to leave for good. And I knew I'd never be able to escape unless I made sure she couldn't get to me. So I did something drastic. I turned her in."

"You reported her to the police?"

Cassandra nodded. "I did it anonymously, but the evidence I gave them was more than enough to convict her. After all, I was her protege. I knew all her secrets. She kept a little black book where she recorded all her dealings, so I stole it and turned it over to the police, along with the details of her biggest crimes. And before I did that, I stole some money from her bank accounts. A small fortune to me, but nothing to her. She didn't even notice it was missing until I was gone, and by then, the police were knocking at her door. She was arrested that very night. And eventually, she was given a 15-year prison sentence.

"I was free. And I had enough money to start over. As far as I was concerned, it was compensation for everything she did to me. I used it to put myself through college and business school, to get my company off the ground. And I used it to build a life for myself that meant I would never, ever have to depend on anyone else. I would never be powerless again."

Mia glanced at Cassandra's face. Her usual stony resolve had returned, her hands steady in her lap.

"Everything that happened with Di? It's why I've spent the last decade focusing on my career, at the expense of relationships. At least, romantic relationships. Because eventually, I found a way to feel empowered again, and that's at the other end of the whip. It satisfies my need for control, along with my other needs. After all, I'm only human. I crave intimacy as much as anyone else. And a part of me simply wants to give others what I needed as a naive young submissive who didn't have anyone to guide her. A part of me wants to be that person for someone else, to make them feel safe, and *loved*, if even just for a night."

There was a yearning in her voice that made Mia's heart ache. And the feeling only deepened when Cassandra turned to look into her eyes.

"So when I saw your auction," she said, "I was drawn to you. I saw you as a younger version of me, someone who needed protecting, someone who needed a Domme to look after them, teach them, in a safe, healthy way. That's why I bid on you, Mia. I wanted to be that person for you."

"And you have been," Mia said. "You've been that, and so much more."

Cassandra shook her head. "No, I haven't. I've failed you. I've been selfish, using you to satisfy my own needs. And I've been too preoccupied with my problems to give you the care and attention you require. I haven't been treating you the way you deserve to be treated. You said so yourself."

Mia winced. *Why do you keep treating me like I'm just your doll?* Those had been her words. Her horrible, horrible words. "I didn't mean it. I didn't mean anything I said."

But Cassandra barely seemed to hear her. "I should have seen it. I should have seen that you were upset—"

"You're not a mind reader, Cassandra. You're not a god. You're only human! You had no way of knowing how I was feeling. You can't blame yourself for something that wasn't your fault."

"You don't understand. As my submissive, you're *my* responsibility. But I'm not fit to be responsible for you, or anyone else! And I never was. I never was." Cassandra trailed off, her shoulders slumping. "Everything that happened with Di? It left me shattered. I've picked up the pieces, but I'm still broken. I can't give you what you need from me. I can't be who you need me to be. Last night was proof enough of that."

"So that's why you want to end this? Because you think you're too broken?"

"It's the truth. I'll only hurt you."

"I'm sorry, Mistress. But that's bullshit." Mia crossed her arms. "You're doing this because you're scared. Sure, maybe you're scared of hurting me. But you're even more scared of giving us a chance. I have feelings for you, and I know you have feelings for me, too. But you've told yourself you're too damaged to be in a relationship, so you're ending things before that can happen."

"That *isn't* true," Cassandra said. "I'm trying to protect you. Because those feelings you have for me, I can never reciprocate them. And stringing you along will only cause you more pain."

"Stop lying to me!"

"I'm not lying to you."

"Then stop lying to yourself! If you really wanted to end things between us? If you really didn't have feelings for me? Why did you tell me all that? Why did you tell me about Diane and everything she did to you? Why did you just pour your heart out to me instead of demanding I leave?"

Mia held Cassandra's gaze, unflinching, unyielding. But inside, her pulse raced, her stomach swimming with nerves. She'd never dared to speak to Cassandra like this before, but she had to get through to her somehow.

But when Cassandra finally spoke, her voice was cold and emotionless. "I thought you deserve to understand why. That's all."

"And I do," Mia said. "I understand that you've been through hell. I understand that everything with Diane left you with deep, painful scars. But you're *not* trying to protect me. You're trying to push me away so you don't have to face the fact that you have feelings for me!"

"That's enough!" Cassandra stood up. "This is *not* a debate. This is *not* a negotiation. It's over, Mia. I took your virginity, which was what I bid for in the first place. As far as I'm concerned, we're done."

"But—"

"I'll pay you what I promised you. Two million dollars, just like we agreed. Since it's such a large sum, it might take a few days to reach you, but it will be in your account by the end of the month. Consider our agreement fulfilled."

Mia's stomach dropped. "Cassandra, please. Please don't do this. Mistress, I l—"

"I am not your Mistress. Not anymore." Cassandra averted her gaze. "Pack your things. You have until this afternoon to leave."

Swallowing the lump in her throat, Mia stood up and went into her bedroom. It wasn't until she'd shut the door firmly behind her that she let her tears fall.

Mistress. I love you. Those were the words she'd been trying to say. That was what she'd wanted to tell her.

Instead, Cassandra had ripped her heart in two.

She choked back a sob, wiping her tears from her cheeks. She wasn't going to waste them on someone who had so cruelly tossed her aside. Cassandra was done with her. So she was done with Cassandra, too.

She marched into the closet and began stuffing her clothes into her suitcase.

CHAPTER 27

"I still don't get why you won't let me drive," Holly said, her arms crossed. "Chelsea's place isn't even that far."

Mia's grip on the steering wheel tightened. "You know you're not allowed to drive at night. Mom said so."

"Mom says a lot of things."

"Well, she's right about this." Mia stopped at the intersection, waiting for the light to turn green. "You just got your permit. You don't have enough experience yet."

"How am I supposed to get experience if I'm never allowed to drive anywhere?"

"Just drop it, Holly! I'm not in the mood to argue with you."

The light turned green, but the car in front of them didn't move. Mia honked her horn until the car drove off.

"What's the matter with you?" Holly said. "You move back home out of nowhere, and you've been acting all crabby since. What gives?"

Mia sighed. "I'm sorry. I don't mean to snap. I've just had a rough few days."

"What happened?"

"It's nothing, really. It's just, I was seeing someone. I really liked her. But she ended things because she didn't want anything serious. It got kind of messy."

"Oh. I'm sorry. What an asshole."

Mia gave her a sharp look. "Language, Holly."

"What a jerk, then. You're too good for her. You should be with someone who treats you right, not someone who plays with your feelings."

"That's just the thing. Before all this, she *did* treat me right. She made me feel special. We had this connection that was unlike anything I've ever felt." Mia shook her head. She didn't need to burden her sister with her problems. "It doesn't matter. She doesn't care about me. She showed me that much. I'm done with her."

So why did she still long for the woman she'd called her Mistress? Why did she feel this pulling inside her chest every time she thought about what they'd shared?

Why did she wish Cassandra would show up at her doorstep, gather her in her arms, and tell her to come home?

"Uh, Mia?" her sister said. "That was Chelsea's house."

"Right. Sorry." Mia did a U-turn, then pulled into Chelsea's driveway. "Have fun at your sleepover."

Holly rolled her eyes. "It's not a sleepover. I'm not ten. We're just hanging out."

"Whatever you say. Do I need to pick you up in the morning?"

Holly shook her head. "Chelsea can drop me off. She has her license already."

Mia nodded. "Don't stay up too late."

"Yes, Mom." Holly got out of the car. "And just so you know, I think it's cool that you like girls. I hope you find one that doesn't suck."

With that, she mumbled a goodbye before bounding up to the front door. As soon as she was inside, Mia pulled out of the driveway and headed back home.

Home. Her real home, not the extravagant penthouse she'd spent almost a month in. To think she'd actually started to feel at home there. To think she'd started to enjoy the life she'd lived with Cassandra. Being treated like a princess. Being showered with expensive things. Being told she deserved it all.

How had she ever believed those words? This was where she belonged. This was the life she'd always known. This was the life she deserved.

She got out of her car and headed to her front door, unlocking it and stepping inside. With her mom at work, the house was empty. She turned on the hallway light and headed to the kitchen to grab something to drink. But as she took a glass from the cupboard, she heard a floorboard creak in the living room.

"Mom? Are you home?"

She waited, but no one answered. Had she imagined the sound? Was it just the old house settling? That had to be it. No one else was home. And the door had been locked when she came in.

So why couldn't she shake the feeling that she wasn't alone?

Another creak, this time from the hallway. She hadn't imagined that one. And it almost sounded like a footstep.

Her heart began to pound. Was there someone in the

house? A burglar? Bruno? Someone sent by his bosses, just like he'd warned her?

Shit. Shit!

She drew in a breath. She didn't have time to panic. She needed to think her way through this. *Get out of here. Get somewhere safe. Call for help.*

She held back a curse. She'd left her phone and keys on the hall table when she came inside. And by the sounds of things, the intruder was out in the hallway, between her and her escape route. She was trapped.

Don't give up yet. Find something to protect yourself with.

She looked around the kitchen, the knife block on the counter catching her eye. But that was too risky. Using a knife for self-defense would be just as dangerous to her as it would be to the intruder.

Instead, she opened a drawer and pulled out a heavy wooden rolling pin, holding it at one end like a bat. Then, taking a deep breath to steel herself, she crept out of the kitchen.

But she didn't make it more than a few steps. Because standing in the middle of the hallway was a woman with a gun in her hand.

And she was pointing it right at Mia.

The woman's lips curled up into a smile. "Hello, Mia."

She froze. *She knows my name.* She had to be one of Bruno's bosses.

But the woman didn't look at all like a criminal. She was well-dressed in a black knee-length coat and heels, with red lipstick and dark, white-streaked hair pulled back into a bun. She hardly seemed the type to carry a gun, let alone use it. But the dark look in her eyes silenced any hope Mia had.

She tightened her grip on the rolling pin, her heart thumping against the inside of her chest. "W-who are you? What do you want?"

"Oh, put that thing down before you hurt yourself." When Mia didn't move, the woman waved the gun toward her. "Go on. Before I lose my patience."

Mia dropped the rolling pin. It hit the ground with a thud. "If this is about the money I owe Bruno—"

"*Owed* Bruno. Put your hands up."

Mia obeyed.

"As I was saying, you don't owe Bruno a thing. Not anymore. You see, I bought your debt from him. So now you owe *me*."

"I can get you your money," Mia said. "I just need a couple of days." Cassandra had promised her it was on the way. And despite everything, Mia trusted her to keep her word. "I'll have it by the end of the month. Bruno gave me until then."

The woman kept the gun fixed on her. "That was between you and Bruno. Now, your debt belongs to me. Now, I *own* you."

"I don't understand. Who *are* you?"

"Ah, how rude of me. I haven't even introduced myself. I know all about you, but you have no idea who I am. My name is Diane. Diane Whiteford."

Mia's stomach dropped. "You're *Di?*" *But how?*

"Oh?" The woman cocked her head to the side. "It seems my reputation precedes me. Did Cassie tell you about me? About us?"

Cassie. Cassandra. This was the woman who had put her through hell.

And now, she had Mia in her clutches.

"W-what do you want from me?" she said. "Why are you doing this?"

"As much as I'd love to answer your questions, I don't have time for that right now. Here's what's going to happen. You're going to come with me. And I'm going to give Cassie a call and see if she'll have a little chat with us. That doesn't sound too bad now, does it?"

Mia stared at her. Was she insane?

"Well? Will you come willingly? Or do I need to shoot you to show you how serious I am? It'll be much harder to get you to the car with a bullet in your leg, but I'll carry you if I have to."

Mia swallowed. Diane was dead serious. "I'll… I'll come with you."

"Good. Come on then."

She stepped forward and grabbed Mia's arm, dragging her toward the front door. As they passed the hall table, Mia glanced at her phone and keys on the tabletop.

Diane followed her gaze. "I'll take that." She grabbed Mia's phone, slipping it into her coat pocket. "Cassandra might not answer my calls, but she'll answer yours."

That may have been true days ago, but now? Cassandra had made it clear she wanted nothing to do with Mia. But Mia didn't tell Diane that. The crazed look in the woman's eyes was a warning not to challenge her.

So she kept her mouth shut as Diane ushered her out the front door, her hand clamped around Mia's arm and the gun at her back. To Diane, she was nothing more than bait.

And Mia prayed to any god that would listen that Cassandra wouldn't get caught in the woman's trap.

CHAPTER 28

Cassandra stared at the glass of wine on the dining room table. The bottle sat beside it. She'd opened it an hour ago, intent on drinking away her troubles.

But she hadn't taken a single sip. Because she didn't want to drown her sorrows. She didn't want to forget how it felt to *hurt*. She wanted to remember it so she'd never make the mistake of being vulnerable again.

Because that was what everything with Mia had been—a mistake. She'd told herself she'd been trying to save Mia from all the bad people out there. She'd told herself she wanted to be the person Mia needed. She'd even told Mia that.

But it was a lie. In truth, Cassandra's motivations had been selfish. She'd been using Mia for her own gain, just like she used everyone in her life. She'd been using Mia to try to heal the wounds Diane had inflicted on her.

But those wounds couldn't be healed. Cassandra would never be whole again.

There was a pounding at her door. She cursed. There

were very few people who had access to her floor, and given how late it was, it was unlikely that maintenance was at her door.

The pounding continued. With an exasperated sigh, she got up and headed to the door, peering through the peephole.

"I know you're in there," Riley said. "Let me in."

Cassandra opened the door. "Do you have any idea what time it is?"

Riley crossed their arms. "Do you? Because you look like you've been wearing those pajamas the entire day. At least."

Cassandra pulled her dressing gown tight around her. "Has something happened with Di?"

"No."

"Then what do you want?"

"Are you going to let me in?"

Cassandra stepped aside. Riley strode past her and into the middle of the penthouse.

"What's going on?" Cassandra said.

"That's what I was going to ask you. Ava called. She said you disappeared from dinner the other day and have been blowing her off ever since. She's worried about you. And frankly, so am I. You haven't left your apartment in *two days*. And you haven't been to the office in two days either. That's enough to make anyone worried."

"Been keeping an eye on me, have you?"

"No, but the security teams here and at your office wouldn't be doing a very good job if they didn't take note of your comings and goings. And they report to me, so I knew something was up. You've been blowing off my calls and messages, too."

"And yet, you didn't take the hint," she murmured.

"Cut the bullshit, Cass. I don't care if you don't want to talk to me. You *owe* me an explanation. I thought something happened to you! I thought Di got to you!"

"Well, she didn't. I'm perfectly fine."

"No, you're not," Riley said. "And I get it. I do. With everything that's happening with Diane—"

"This isn't about Di. At least, not in the way you think."

"Is it about Mia, then?"

She stared at Riley. "How do you know about Mia?"

"Once again, you hired me to handle security for you. I wouldn't be doing my job very well if I didn't know who you've been in contact with. And Mia Brooks has been living with you for the last month. At least, until yesterday morning, when she left the building with a suitcase in tow. She hasn't been back since."

Cassandra sighed.

Riley sat down on the arm of the couch. "Come on. What happened?"

Cassandra collapsed onto the couch. She closed her eyes. And she told Riley everything.

About Mia. About their arrangement, and the way the lines had blurred. About her relationship with Diane, and how it had left her too broken to ever be with anyone again.

About how she'd pushed Mia away, all for her own good.

And when she finished speaking, she couldn't look Riley in the eye. Because saying everything out loud had forced her to face the truth.

She hadn't pushed Mia away to protect her. She'd done it to protect herself. Because she couldn't handle being broken again.

Silence stretched between them. And with it, the guilt inside her grew and grew until there was no room for anything else.

Riley broke the silence. "Do you remember what I said the other day? When I told you why I decided to take that first job with you?"

"You said it was because you saw something in me. You saw someone who had darkness in their past, but had overcome it." Cassandra shook her head. "But that was just an illusion. I never escaped my past. I just thought I had."

"I've thought the same thing at low points in my life," Riley said. "No matter how hard we try, our pasts will always be with us, whispering into our ears, reminding us of what used to be. That's something we can't control. But what we *can* control is our choices. We can choose our future, our present. And you've already done that, Cassandra. When you helped Kimberly back then, you chose. When you started the Queens Club, you chose. Every favor, every gift, every time you've helped someone, you chose to believe that there was good in the world. You chose to overcome everything you've been through. And you can do it again."

"It's just not that simple."

"No, it's not. But it's worth it. The fight is always worth it. Don't let your past hold you hostage. Don't let Diane hold you hostage." Riley put their hand on her shoulder. "Just think about it, okay?"

Cassandra nodded. "I will."

Riley stood up. "I'll give you some space. And call Ava back before she reports you missing."

Cassandra led Riley to the door and opened it up. "I

never told you that I talked to Kimberly recently. She's doing well now. Found herself a rich suitor. They're married and have another kid together."

"Good for her," Riley said. "After what she's been through, she deserves a happy life. And so do you."

With a nod of farewell, they disappeared toward the elevator.

Cassandra went back inside, silence hanging heavily in the air. Since Mia left, her apartment seemed too quiet, too empty, echoing the way Cassandra felt inside.

Empty. Alone. She'd always felt that way. But it wasn't until Mia came into her life that she realized it. She had it all. Money. Power. Security. But the life she'd led to get to where she was? The sacrifices she'd made? They'd stopped her from truly living.

But Mia had reminded her what it was like to live, really *live*. And if that wasn't worth fighting for? If that wasn't worth risking everything for? What was the point of it all?

Riley was right. After all this time, Cassandra was still letting Diane hold her hostage, still letting her control her. *Never again.* That was the promise she'd made herself. That was the choice she'd made. It had dictated her every decision for the past 12 years.

But today, she was choosing to let go of the past and follow her heart.

She took her phone from the coffee table and dialed Mia's number.

When Mia picked up, Cassandra didn't give her a chance to speak. "I'm so sorry, Mia. I'm sorry about everything. I need to tell you—"

"Cassie. How lovely to hear from you."

Cassandra froze. That was Diane's voice. What was she doing with Mia's phone?

Her stomach lurched. *Mia. She has Mia.*

"I was just about to call you, if you can believe that," Diane said. "I just needed to persuade Mia here to unlock her phone."

"You're lying. This is just another trick."

"I assure you, Mia is right here with me. Here, I'll put her on."

The line went silent. Then, Mia's voice rang out through the phone. "Cassandra, don't listen to her. This is a trap—"

"That's enough!" Diane's voice now, sharp and firm. She cleared her throat. "I apologize. She's a bit of a feisty one. I can see why you like—"

"Give me one reason I shouldn't call the police right now," Cassandra said.

"Because then you'll never see Mia again. Not alive, anyway."

Cassandra held back a curse. Diane didn't make idle threats. She knew that from experience. "What do you want?"

"I've already told you what I want. I want you to pay for what you did. You see, I've found your weakness, Cassie. The one thing you care about the most. It's not your company. It's not even your precious Queens Club. I thought it was, but I was wrong. Your Achilles heel is the pretty little thing I have sitting right next to me."

Was Diane right? All along, Cassandra had thought that the Queens Club was the thing she valued the most too. But somewhere along the line, that changed. Somewhere along the line, Mia had become the most precious thing in the world to her.

How had Diane known it when Cassandra hadn't even figured it out herself?

"And now," Diane continued, "Mia is mine. You see, I bought her debt. I *own* her."

Cassandra's stomach iced over. "What do you want with her?" A thousand possibilities raced through Cassandra's mind, each worse than the last. "If you hurt her... If you so much as touch her—"

"Oh, Cassie. You have this all wrong. I don't want to hurt her. I simply want to make a trade. Her, for you. Come to me, and I'll let her go."

"All right," Cassandra said. "Where are you?"

"I'm not stupid. I'm not going to let you lead the police to me."

The police weren't who Cassandra had in mind. "Then what? What do you want to do?"

"We'll meet somewhere. Just the three of us. How about... the Queens Club?"

The Queens Club? Why would Diane want to meet there?

"Of course, it's crawling with security guards since you tightened things up after I dropped off my little gift. You'll have to call them off."

"I can do that," Cassandra said.

"You *will* do that."

"I will. You have my word."

"Good. Clear the place out. Tell security and everyone else to leave. Then meet me there at midnight. And Cassie?"

"Yes?" she replied.

"If you try anything, if you call the police or leave

anyone lurking nearby to come to your rescue, I'll blow Mia's brains out. And I'm sure you remember that I always keep my word."

"I won't try anything."

"Then we'll see you at midnight."

Cassandra hung up the phone, hands shaking with fury and fear. *Mia. She has Mia.*

But she couldn't afford to fall apart now. There was only an hour until midnight. She had to call off security and clear the building.

She dialed Riley's number.

"I need you to do something for me," she said as soon as they answered. "I can't explain why. I just need you to trust me."

"What is it?" Riley asked.

"I need you to clear out the Queens Club. If there are any members still inside, I need them out. And I need you to call off security and shut down the alarm system. Do you understand?"

"What? No, I don't. What's going on?"

"I told you, I can't explain why. I just need you to do as I say. I'm ordering you to do as I say."

Riley paused. "Are you saying that as my employer or as a friend?"

Cassandra gritted her teeth. "I'm speaking to you as your employer. Now go. And let me know when you've carried out my instructions."

"Message received. I'll be in touch when it's done." Without another word, Riley hung up the phone.

Cassandra pushed down the guilt gnawing inside her chest. She'd never played that card with Riley before, but what choice did she have? She'd make it up to them after this was all over, assuming she survived whatever Diane had waiting for her.

Because she was walking into a trap. She knew it. She knew how much Diane wanted to make her hurt. But she couldn't let Mia be collateral. She needed to get her out of Diane's hands.

And she'd risk anything to do that.

CHAPTER 29

"There." Diane tugged at the ropes around Mia's wrists, testing her knots. "How does that feel?"

Mia glanced over her shoulder at Diane, who stood behind the chair. "A little tight, actually."

"Now, don't lie to me. Do you think I don't know how to tie someone up properly? Where do you think Cassie learned it? I taught her everything she knows." Diane drew a finger down Mia's cheek. *"Everything."*

Mia shrank back, but there was nowhere to go. Not only were her wrists tied behind the backrest of the chair, but her legs were tied to the chair too. She could barely move.

Which was probably why Diane felt secure enough to set her gun down on the bar nearby. That was a good sign. She was letting her guard down. If Mia could distract her somehow, maybe she'd be able to escape before Cassandra came. She didn't know what time it was, but it had to be getting close to midnight. She couldn't let Cassandra walk into this trap.

"I-I still don't understand," Mia said, trying to sound as

scared as she could. Maybe that would garner some sympathy from Diane. "Where are we? Why did you bring me here?"

"Really? Cassandra didn't tell you about her precious Queens Club?" Diane crouched down beside Mia's chair. "Makes me wonder what else she hasn't told you."

"She doesn't tell me *anything*. I think you have the wrong idea about us. We're not together. We just had an arrangement. And it's all over now."

"Enough with the lies, Mia. You can't fool me."

"It's the truth. She's paying me. I needed some quick money, so I auctioned myself off, and she won."

"That's how you met? She bought you at an auction?" Diane laughed. "That's quite the love story. It's almost impossible to believe."

Mia shook her head. "We're not in love."

"Oh, please. I saw you together at that restaurant. I saw the way she acted with you. She loves you. It was obvious just watching the two of you."

"That's not true. She doesn't love me. She doesn't have any feelings for me at all."

"Deny it all you want. I know the truth. And the fact that she's coming here for you in the first place is proof enough. She has to know she's walking into a trap. She wouldn't risk her life for just anyone."

Mia's stomach sank. "What are you planning to do to her?"

"Oh, you'll find out soon enough. In fact, you'll have a front-row seat to the show. Speaking of which, I should prepare."

"Prepare for what?" Mia pulled at the ropes around her wrists. "What are you going to do?"

But Diane didn't answer her. Instead, she went over to the bar and picked up a large plastic container with a handle and a screw-on lid. She'd carried it with her when she marched Mia into the club, along with a small duffel bag containing the ropes she'd used to tie Mia up.

At the time, Mia had been too distracted by the gun sticking into her back to worry about what the container held. But as soon as Diane unscrewed the lid, the smell of its contents hit her.

Gas. The container was full of gasoline.

Diane tossed the lid aside and began pouring gas over the bar top.

"What are you doing?" Mia yelled.

"I told you. I'm preparing for Cassie's arrival." The bar now covered in gasoline, Diane moved on to the rest of the room, spreading gas over and around the furniture. "She'll be here soon. And once she gets here, I'm going to burn this place down."

"What? No!" Mia struggled against her restraints. "This is crazy. You can't do this!"

"I can, and I will. It's the only way to make things right. Cassandra took everything from me. So I'm going to take everything from her."

Fear surged through Mia's body. "Please. Please don't do this!"

Diane stopped mid-pour and returned to Mia's chair. "I'm sorry. Really. You're innocent in all this, I know that. But I need to do this."

Mia trembled, her head spinning from the thick gasoline fumes. "Why?"

"I don't expect you to understand. You love her, so you could never fathom how badly she hurt me. She was *mine*. She belonged to *me*. But she betrayed me. She needs to be punished."

A chill rolled down Mia's spine. Diane wanted to punish her? That was what this all came down to? Not revenge but control?

That was what she was willing to kill over?

Diane patted Mia on the shoulder. "Sit tight while I finish this, will you?"

Gas can in hand, she headed to the doorway and out into the hall, leaving a trail of gasoline behind her.

Mia's heart thundered in her chest. She looked frantically around the room for anything that could help her, but nothing was within reach. Could she shuffle her chair over to the bar and grab something? Could she loosen the ropes enough to free herself somehow? Maybe if she had more time. But she could hear Diane's footsteps. She was already on her way back.

Mia glanced up at the fire sprinklers on the roof. Would they be enough to stop the blaze?

Diane appeared in the doorway. "I disabled the sprinklers already. They're not going to save you. No one can. Not even Cassandra." Tossing the now-empty gas can aside, she strode over to Mia and leaned in close, hot breath burning her face. "She needs to pay for what she did to me. She's going to burn. And while she burns, she's going to watch you burn, too."

"Please!" Tears filled Mia's eyes. "Please don't do this…"

She peered up at Diane, searching her face for any hint of mercy. But all she saw was hate. Cold, hard *hate*.

"I'm sorry, Mia. But this is how it has to—"

From the front of the building came the loud creak of the heavy entrance doors.

Mia's heart stopped. *Cassandra. She's here.*

"Cassandra, no!" she screamed. "Get out of—"

Her words were cut off by a piece of cloth shoved into her mouth by Diane. "Shut up. And if you try anything, I'll kill her the moment she walks through this door."

Mia fell silent. She was dead either way. There was nothing she could do but await her fate.

Moments later, Cassandra appeared in the doorway. Mia's stomach dropped. There was no escape for either of them now.

"Oh, Mia." Cassandra rushed toward her. "Thank god you're—"

"Hold it!" Diane said.

Cassandra stopped in her tracks. Mia turned to look at Diane, her heart in her throat. The woman stood behind her chair, holding something in her hand. But it wasn't the gun.

It was a match.

"Not. Another. Step," Diane said.

Cassandra held up her hands, her eyes flickering between the puddles of gasoline around the room. "All right. Just don't do anything rash."

"Rash? *Rash?*" Diane laughed. "I'm holding a match in a room covered in gasoline. Do you really think I haven't thought this through? Do you think I haven't been planning this for twelve long years?"

"Let's just talk about this."

"You already made yourself clear. You're done talking with me. The time for talk is over. Now, it's time to act."

"Wait!" Cassandra stepped forward, then stopped herself. "I came to you, just like I promised. Just like you wanted. So let Mia go."

"I'm afraid I can't do that."

Cassandra's face fell. "Di, please. This is between you and me. Mia has nothing to do with this."

"Yes, and it's a pity. This is such a waste of her potential. She would have been perfect for the work we did all those years ago. But, unfortunately for her, she's the thing you care about the most. This club is the second. So I thought, why not kill two birds with one stone? Destroy the only two things in the world that you love?"

"Diane, please," Cassandra said. "Just let her go. I'll do anything you want. I can give you your life back. I can give you enough money to start over anywhere in the world. I'll even come with you. We can be together again. Just let Mia go."

"I'm sorry, Cassie. There's nothing you can say, nothing you can do, that will ever make up for what you did to me. Consider this your final punishment."

"Wait! If you light this fire, you won't have time to get out of here. You'll die here too."

"Do you think I care?" Diane screamed. "Do you think I care whether I live or die? What's the point of living when I have nothing left?"

The anguish in the woman's voice pierced through to Mia's soul. There was no arguing with her. She was determined to go out in a blaze of glory, taking both of them with her.

Mia's breaths grew heavy in her chest. *This is it. This is really it.*

"Don't do this," Cassandra pleaded.

"I wish I didn't have to. But this is the only way you'll learn. We're all going to burn together."

It happened faster than Mia could blink.

Diane struck the match against the back of the chair.

Cassandra lunged toward her.

The lit match flew from Diane's hand, landing in a puddle of gasoline.

And the room went up in flames.

CHAPTER 30

Cassandra crashed into Diane, sending her tumbling to the ground. She fell down with her, only just managing to scramble away from the rapidly spreading fire beside them.

But so did Diane. She grabbed onto Cassandra's ankles and pulled her toward her. "You can't get away, Cassie. Not this time."

Cassandra kicked at her frantically. But Diane held on, her arms wrapped around Cassandra's legs, her eyes dark and crazed.

She's insane. She's gone insane.

Cassandra looked around. The flames were spreading fast. She needed to get Diane off her. She needed to get Mia out of here.

There! Stretching her arm out, she grabbed the leg of a nearby barstool and dragged it toward them. She gave it a shove, tipping it in Diane's direction. Gravity took care of the rest, sending the heavy stool toppling down onto Diane's head.

She grunted, her grip on Cassandra's legs weakening.

Now's my chance! She pulled her legs from Diane's grasp and kicked at her, hard. The first two kicks battered uselessly at her shoulders. But the third? It hit Diane square in the face, snapping her head back against the bottom of the bar behind her with a sickening thud.

The woman slumped to the floor. She was out cold, or worse. But Cassandra didn't have time to check. She needed to free Mia.

Rising to her feet among the flames, she rushed over to Mia's chair, pulling the cloth from her mouth and taking her tear-stained face in her hands. "Are you okay? I'm going to get you out of here, all right?"

Mia nodded. Cassandra rounded the chair and started working at the knots around Mia's wrists. But they were tied tightly. It would take too long to undo them. And the fire was spreading fast. They were running out of time.

Cassandra looked around. There was a fire extinguisher beside the bar, but it would be useless against the flames. She glanced up at the ceiling. She could hardly see it through the smoke. "Why aren't the fire sprinklers turning on?"

"Diane disabled them," Mia said. "She—" Her words were cut off by a fit of coughing.

Cassandra cursed. They needed to get out of here. "I need a knife. I'll be right back."

She rushed over to the bar and reached behind it, grabbing a sharp paring knife and returning to Mia's chair. Not a moment later, flames swooped along the bar top, setting it alight.

That was close. Taking the knife, Cassandra sawed at the ropes around Mia's wrists. *Come on. Come on... Yes!*

The ropes came free. She moved on to Mia's ankles, making quick work of the ropes there too.

Now to get out of here. Taking Mia in her arms, she drew her to her feet. "Are you all right? Can you walk?"

Mia's answer was a nod and a cough. The room was filled with smoke now, and Cassandra could barely see the exit. But she knew the layout of the bar and the rest of the club well enough to navigate it with her eyes closed.

"Let's get out of—"

A loud crash erupted behind them. They ducked down, Cassandra covering Mia's body with her own. The liquor bottles behind the bar had begun to explode, fanning the flames even further.

"Come on," Cassandra said. "Hurry!"

"But..." Mia glanced toward Diane, who lay unconscious on the floor.

"Forget her. We need to go."

With one arm around Mia, both to support her and keep her from getting lost in the smoke, they made their way out of the bar and into the hallway. But Diane had been thorough. The fire had already spread out to the hall, and it was rapidly filling with smoke.

"This way," Cassandra said. "Quickly."

She led Mia toward the entrance. But as they approached the front doors, they found their path cut off by a wall of flames.

"No!" She yanked Mia backward as the flames whooshed toward them. They weren't getting out that way.

But the hallway they'd come down had been completely overtaken by flames. They couldn't go back either.

Shit. Shit! Cassandra rubbed her eyes. They were gritty with smoke, and she could barely see a thing through the haze. As Mia coughed beside her, Cassandra began to cough too. Her lungs burned, and she was starting to feel lightheaded. She needed to close her eyes, just for a moment—

Focus, Cassandra! She ducked down beneath the worst of the smoke, pulling Mia down with her, and looked around. There was a fire door nearby in an alcove on the left side of the foyer. They could escape through that.

But they had to find it first. And there was so much smoke, and they'd gotten turned around, and she didn't know which way was which. And it was getting harder and harder to breathe—

She collapsed onto her knees.

"Cassandra!" Mia cried.

"I'm here." Cassandra reached for her, grabbing hold of her hand. "I'm right here."

Summoning all her strength, she pulled herself to her feet. She couldn't give up now. Not when they were so close.

"There's a fire exit to the side. We'll head for that." She put her arm around Mia's shoulder. "Hold on to me. We're going to get out of here."

Mia grabbed hold of Cassandra's waist, clinging tightly to her. Crouching down again, Cassandra led her blindly through the smoke.

But it was futile. She didn't know where they were going. She couldn't see a thing. They were trapped.

They were going to die here.

She blinked the tears out of her smoke-filled eyes. "I'm sorry, Mia. For everything."

"Cassandra—"

"No. You were right. You need to know that you were right about everything. And I need to tell you…"

She took Mia by the shoulders, steadying herself. She could barely stand, barely breathe.

But if she had to, she would use her last breath to tell Mia how she felt.

"I need to tell you that I—"

"Cassandra!"

Cassandra blinked. Was that Riley's voice? Or was she hearing things?

"Cass?" The voice again, somewhere in the distance. "Are you in there?"

"Riley?" She shook her head, attempting to clear it. The voice—it was real! "Riley, we're in here. We can't get out."

Riley cursed. "I can't see you through all the smoke. I'm near the fire exit. Just follow my voice!"

The fire exit. Their way out.

She took Mia's hand. "Come on. Let's get out of here."

Once again, she began pulling Mia blindly through the smoke. But this time, she had Riley's voice to guide her. She closed her eyes, holding Mia's hand tightly, dragging her along, dragging her own flagging body along with what little strength she had left.

"Come on!" Riley said. "You're close now."

There. Riley's silhouette in the smoke-filled doorway. And Cassandra had never been more grateful to see it.

She stumbled toward them, Mia in tow, her hand outstretched—

"Got you!" Riley grabbed onto Cassandra's forearm, then Mia's, pulling them both through the door. They staggered down the steps, the cold night air hitting them. Riley dragged them away from the door, clear of the blazing building and the smoke billowing from it.

Cassandra collapsed onto the cold, hard concrete, Mia in her arms. They coughed and spluttered, breathing clean air deep into their burning lungs.

They were safe. They were finally safe.

∽

Cassandra sat on the stretcher, holding an oxygen mask to her face. On another stretcher nearby, Mia was being examined by a paramedic. Both of them had a case of smoke inhalation and would need to go to the hospital for observation, but otherwise, they were none the worse for wear.

Luck had been on their side tonight. They were safe. They were unharmed. Cassandra couldn't say the same for the Queens Club. The fire had been put out, and the building would need serious repairs. But it was still standing.

So was she. And so was Mia. That was what mattered.

And they had Riley to thank for it. Cassandra glanced over to where they stood nearby, wrapping up a conversation with a pair of police officers. As the officers walked away, Riley returned to Cassandra's side.

"How are you doing?" they asked.

"I've had better days, but I've had worse, too." Cassandra inhaled deeply through her mask. "You have no idea how glad I am that you showed up."

"That's what friends are for."

Cassandra grimaced. "About that. I'm sorry for ordering you around the way I did. I can't say I've ever been so grateful that someone disobeyed my orders."

"Well, I did obey them at first. I cleared out the club, just like you told me to, but I couldn't ignore the signs that something was seriously wrong. So I came back and hid out of sight, watching the club. I saw you go inside. And when smoke started pouring out of the building, I knew you were in trouble, so I called 911 and stepped in."

"Thank you, Riley. I'll never be able to repay you for what you did tonight."

They put a hand on Cassandra's shoulder. "Don't sweat it. Just try not to get into any situations like that again, okay?"

Cassandra nodded. "I'll do my best."

"We found someone!" yelled a firefighter standing in the doorway to the club. "We need medical."

Cassandra exchanged a glance with Riley. *Diane?* When the authorities arrived, Cassandra had told them Diane was still in the building, along with everything else that had transpired, but it had been too dangerous for anyone to enter the club until the fire was out.

Riley tipped their head toward the club. "I'll go find out what's happening."

Riley slipped seamlessly into the crowd of emergency responders gathered near the club's entrance. Not a moment later, a firefighter emerged from the building carrying Diane. She was so covered in ash and smoke that Cassandra barely recognized her. Had she survived, somehow?

"She's still breathing," the fireman said. "Where's medical?"

The paramedic examining Mia handed her an oxygen mask and told her not to move, grabbing his bag and rushing off toward the building. As she held the mask up to her mouth, she glanced in Cassandra's direction. Since escaping the burning club, they hadn't had a chance to say more than a few words to each other. And there was so much Cassandra needed to say to her.

Removing her oxygen mask, she got up from her stretcher and made her way over to Mia, taking a seat beside her.

"Are you sure that's okay?" Mia said, eying the discarded oxygen mask on Cassandra's stretcher.

"I don't care if it is or not. I needed to talk to you. There's so much I have to tell you."

"I have so much to say to you too, but I…" Mia lowered her mask to her lap. "I don't even know where to begin. I'm still trying to wrap my head around everything that's happened."

"Oh, Mia. I'm so sorry. I'm sorry I let Diane get her hands on you. I promise you, she won't be able to hurt you again." Cassandra glanced toward the entrance to the building, where Diane was being transferred onto a stretcher. "If she survives this, she'll be going right back to prison. I'll make sure of it. After what she did to you, I'll make sure she pays the price."

Mia shook her head. "No. No more revenge. No more punishing anyone. That's what got us into this mess in the first place."

"All right. But Diane needs to be locked up somewhere she can't hurt anyone. And I'll make sure that happens."

Mia nodded. "Thank you. For rescuing me and all."

"I don't deserve your thanks. I'm the reason you needed rescuing in the first place. But even if it wasn't my fault, I would have come for you. I'd have moved heaven and earth to get to you. Besides, I should be thanking *you*."

Mia tilted her head. "For what?"

"For everything. You have no idea what you've done for me. No idea how much you've changed me." Cassandra closed her eyes, letting her head fall back. "The reason we met? The reason I bid on your auction? It was to save you. All along, I was trying to save you. But it was me who needed saving."

She turned to Mia. Mia was looking back at her like she'd gone crazy from the lack of oxygen.

And maybe she had. Or maybe she was finally allowing herself to feel all the things she'd been afraid to feel.

"I needed to be saved from myself," Cassandra said. "From all my fears and doubts. From the walls I'd built to protect myself. But you saved me from all of that. You saved me from the prison I'd built around my heart."

"Cassandra, I… I don't know what to say."

"Then listen. Listen while I tell you how I feel about you. All this time, I've been so afraid to face my feelings. I once promised myself I'd never trust anyone again, never make myself vulnerable to anyone again. I've been holding on to that like a shield to protect me from getting hurt. But instead, I was letting my past control me." Cassandra took Mia's hands in hers. "So now, I'm choosing to follow my heart. I love you, Mia."

Mia drew her hands back, only to throw her arms around Cassandra's neck. "I love you too."

Cassandra's heart surged. She reached up, cupped Mia's face in her hands, and pressed her lips to Mia's in a tender kiss. It drew on and on, flooding Cassandra with warmth and light, until the events of the past few hours were just a blemish on a clear, starlit sky.

Mia murmured into her lips, pulling back slightly. "Wow. That was…" She let out a soft breath. "I think I'm a little dizzy."

"Here." Cassandra picked up the oxygen mask from Mia's lap and held it up to her. "I don't want to have to explain to the paramedics that I kissed you so hard you passed out."

With a smile, Mia took the oxygen mask from her and strapped it onto her face, leaning her head on Cassandra's shoulder.

Cassandra wrapped an arm around her, pulling her close. "Rest now. I'll take care of you."

CHAPTER 31

Mia glanced at the clock on the oven as she pulled the pie crust out. Cassandra would be home any minute now.

Right on cue, the front door to the penthouse opened. Mia left the kitchen, meeting Cassandra by the door.

"Welcome home, Mistress." Mia planted a kiss on her cheek. "How was your day?"

"Long." Cassandra slipped off her heels and hung up her coat. "I stopped by the Queens Club before work this morning to meet with some contractors about repairing the damage caused by the fire. Given how old the building is, it would be simpler to knock it down and rebuild. But there's so much history there. I'm going to save as much of it as I can, no matter the cost."

"I'm glad it can be saved. I know how much the Queens Club means to you."

"Yes, but in the end, it's only a building. The relationships formed there are what's really important." Cassandra led her over to the couch. "Sit with me."

Mia took a seat beside her. They'd slipped so easily back into their life of domesticity. "Is there anything I can do for you? A drink, maybe?"

"No, but you can tell me all about your day. Weren't you catching up with your family today?"

Mia nodded. "I took Mom and Holly out for lunch. I stopped by the house afterward too. It feels like forever since I've been back there."

In the aftermath of that night at the Queens Club, Mia hadn't wanted to leave Cassandra alone. While they'd both been released from the hospital the next day, it had taken them longer to fully recover. Because while the physical effects of their ordeal had only lingered for a few days, the events of that night had taken a significant mental and emotional toll on them both, especially Cassandra. She would never admit it, but Mia could tell.

So she'd stayed by her Mistress's side, day after day, until Cassandra was her usual self again. And before they knew it, Mia had spent another month living in Cassandra's apartment. Then one day, Cassandra asked her to stay for good.

"So?" Cassandra said. "Did you tell them you're moving in?"

Mia nodded.

"How did they take it?"

"Well, I think. They were both pretty surprised. I mean, it's only been a month since I told them that the woman I've been seeing all this time is you. They were pretty shocked about that, and even then they still think I was working as your maid. But I think they're on board now. Holly thinks you're great, and Mom just said if I'm happy, she's happy."

"And are you?" Cassandra asked. "Happy?"

"Yes, Mistress. You make me happy."

Cassandra kissed Mia's forehead, then placed a hand on hers. "There's something I should tell you. It's about Diane."

Mia's stomach flipped. "What is it?"

"My sources at the hospital have given me an update. She's awake. Stable. But she's in rough shape. Most of her body is covered in third-degree burns. It'll be a long time before she's discharged, and even then, she'll be dealing with lifelong effects. Once she's well enough, she'll stand trial. The charges are solid. She's facing life in prison."

"Huh. That's a lot to take in." Mia shook her head. "It's crazy, but I'm glad she survived. Even *she* didn't deserve to die in such a horrible way. But she definitely deserves to be locked up for good."

"For now, she's under guard at the hospital. She can't exactly go anywhere in her condition, but she's being watched closely. She's not a threat anymore."

"How do you feel about all this?" While Mia had some strong feelings toward Diane, none of them positive, the woman had tormented Cassandra for half her life.

"I feel... at peace." Cassandra closed her eyes, exhaling softly. "It's hard to believe it, but after all this time, I'm free of her. I'm finally free." She wrapped her arm around Mia, drawing her close. "It's such a relief to have all of our problems behind us."

Mia murmured in agreement. It wasn't only Diane who was out of the picture. All Mia's problems were solved, too. The morning she left the hospital, she'd found two million dollars waiting for her in her bank account, which she immediately used to pay off all her family's debts. Her sister's medical bills. Her mom's credit cards. The mortgage on the house their father had bought them before he died.

Of course, Cassandra had offered to pay off all those debts for her, but Mia had turned her down. She wanted to take care of them all herself, to wipe the slate clean and start fresh. She'd even tried to pay Bruno back, but he told her that after selling her debt to Diane, Mia didn't owe him anything. She didn't owe *anyone* anything.

She was free now, too.

And she still had plenty of money left over, even after setting aside enough to put Holly through college. She'd set aside enough to put herself through college too, if she ever decided to go. But life had taken her in a different direction. She was on a new path now, one dictated not by the needs of others but by her own. It was a path of her choosing.

And while she didn't know which way to go next, with Cassandra at her side, she had no doubt that she'd figure it out.

Cassandra glanced toward the kitchen with furrowed brows. "Is that dinner I smell? Because I told you not to cook tonight. I told you we're ordering in so we can enjoy the evening together without you running off to the kitchen every five minutes."

Mia peered up at Cassandra from under her eyelashes. "You said not to cook dinner. You didn't say anything about dessert."

"Really?" Cassandra shook her head. "I suppose I can let it slide, just this once. You're *very* lucky your cooking is excellent."

"I'm just lucky I have a girlfriend who appreciates it."

Cassandra stretched out beside her, draping an arm over

the back of the couch. "So, after dinner. After dessert. We have the rest of the night free. Not to mention the whole weekend." She turned to Mia, a gleam in her eye. "Whatever shall we do with ourselves?"

Mia bit her lip, every sinful possibility playing in her mind. "Whatever you want, Mistress."

"I have a better idea. You see, I've been doing some thinking. And I've realized I need to do better at making sure your needs are being met."

"Oh, they definitely are. You've made sure of that." Multiple times a day, sometimes.

Cassandra placed her hand on Mia's leg. "Nevertheless, I want to give you the freedom to explore your desires. I want you to feel comfortable enough in your desires to tell me what you need. And, more importantly, I want you to have choices."

Freedom. Choices. Her entire life, she'd been denied both. Now, the future held endless possibilities.

And so did tonight.

"I'll let you choose what we do tonight," Cassandra said, sliding her hand up Mia's thigh. "That is, as long as it involves me fucking you until you beg for more."

Mia's lips parted, a short, sharp breath escaping them. Now that sex was on the table, her Mistress didn't hesitate to be direct with her. In fact, she seemed to delight in the way it made Mia tremble and blush. She was no more immune to Cassandra's gaze, her voice, her touch, than she'd been the night they met.

"What's it going to be, Mia? What do *you* want?"

"Well, I..." Up until now, it had been Cassandra holding the reins, teaching her, guiding her through a world she'd only ever dreamed about, giving her the chance to explore every facet of her sexuality.

But there were still so many things they hadn't done together. Still so many things Mia wanted to experience.

Perhaps, tonight, they could start with just one.

"There is something I've always wanted to try…"

CHAPTER 32

Cassandra pulled Mia's wrists above her head, binding them together and tying them to the headboard. "Now there's no getting out of this for you."

Mia squirmed on the bed, testing her bonds. This wasn't the thing she'd asked Cassandra to do, but her Mistress never missed an opportunity to tie her up.

Especially now that she'd converted the guest room Mia had spent her first month in into a playroom. It was outfitted with every erotic tool and toy she could dream of. Nowadays, they spent more nights in the playroom than in their bedroom.

Cassandra gave her a sharp slap on the side of her ass cheek. "Stop wriggling about."

Mia obeyed.

Her Mistress drew her hand down Mia's side, tracing the curve of her waist and hip. "Now that I have you where I want you, I'm going to have a little fun."

Heat rose to her skin. Cassandra had ordered her to

strip down to her panties before tying her up. Already, Mia wished she would rip them off.

Instead, Cassandra climbed onto the bed and threw one leg over her, straddling her body. Mia gazed up at her, enthralled. After all this time, the sight of her Mistress still took her breath away. Her long, wavy hair cascaded down her shoulders like a curtain of silk, her lips an alluring crimson. And all she wore was an enticingly short negligee made of black silk edged with ivory lace.

She dragged a fingertip down the center of Mia's chest. "Now, let's get you warmed up."

She dipped low, her lips grazing Mia's cheek, sweeping down the side of her throat, her breast. She took a nipple in her mouth and sucked it firmly, snaking her hand up to Mia's other nipple and rolling it between her fingertips, sending jolts of electricity through Mia's body.

"Oh!" Her chest arched, pushing back against Cassandra. She didn't need warming up. She'd been wet and ready the moment they walked into the room.

But her Mistress was in charge. And if she wanted to torment Mia with her touch, ravish her with her lips and tongue, rain pleasures all over her body until she begged for mercy?

What choice did Mia have but to accept her exquisite fate?

She closed her eyes, sinking deeper into the bed. Her Mistress's lips traveled down her stomach, down to her panties. She pulled the waistband down slightly, painting kisses atop each of Mia's hipbones and the base of her belly, but no lower. Not where Mia really wanted her.

She whimpered. "Please..."

Cassandra kissed her way down the front of Mia's thigh as she peeled her panties down, past her hips, her knees, her ankles, lips following in their wake. Tossing the panties aside, she kissed her way back up Mia's other leg, slowly, painstakingly. Up the inside of her calf. Up her inner thigh. All the while, Mia trembled and moaned, yearning, *aching* for more.

She spread her legs even wider. "Please, Mistress. *Please.*"

Cassandra's lips crept up the inside of her thigh, kissing and sucking the sensitive, rarely touched skin there, until finally, they reached the point where her thighs met. Parting Mia's lips with her tongue, she ran it up and down her folds gently.

Mia's head tipped back, her body slackening. "Mm, yes..."

But 'gently' was as far as her Mistress would go. She feathered her tongue over Mia's clit with infuriating lightness, dipped it into her entrance teasingly. And while Mia crept closer and closer to the edge, the release she sought was just out of reach.

"Mistress..." Her hands pulled at the ropes binding them. "Can you let me come? Please?"

"Not yet." Cassandra straightened up. "Like I said, that was only the warm-up. Now it's time for the main event."

Mia's heart raced. She already knew what was coming. But that did little to settle her nerves.

On her knees between Mia's legs, Cassandra took the hem of her negligee and pulled it up over her head, dropping it to the bed beside them. Underneath, her breasts were bare. But around her waist was a leather strap-on harness, a sleek black dildo jutting out from in front of it.

A thrill rose through Mia's body. This was what she'd asked her Mistress for. This had been her one request.

"But are you *really* ready for me?" Cassandra reached between Mia's legs, sliding her fingers down to her entrance. "You're certainly wet enough."

Mia exhaled sharply. "I'm ready. Please!"

"Please, who?" Cassandra asked firmly.

"Please, Mistress. I *need* you."

She screwed her eyes shut, pleading silently. Not a moment later, something hard pressed between her legs, sliding down to her entrance.

She tensed.

"Relax," Cassandra commanded. "You need to let me in."

Mia tried her hardest to obey, but her body refused to listen to her. Her anxious excitement had her on edge.

Cassandra drew a hand down Mia's cheek. "Close your eyes. Imagine we're back in that chateau in the mountains, back in that room where I tied you up and flogged you until you forgot your own name."

Desire swelled in Mia's center. How could she forget that night?

"Remember what that felt like," Cassandra whispered. "Remember the way your body yielded to her Mistress. Embrace that feeling. Give in to it."

Mia drew in a breath and closed her eyes, recalling how it had felt that night to let go. To surrender to sensation, to surrender to her Mistress's will so completely that she lost herself. She sank into that feeling, the touch of Cassandra's hands on her skin, the weight of her body, the press of the strap between her legs.

"Good girl," her Mistress said. "Just like that."

Ever so slowly, Cassandra slipped inside her. Mia let out a shuddering gasp as Cassandra buried herself deep, filling her completely. Then, she began to move inside her, slowly at first, then faster. A moan slid from Mia's lips, the fire inside her flaring.

"That's it," Cassandra said. "Yield to me."

Mia's head fell back, her hips rising from the bed. She wrapped her fingers around the rope above her head, bracing herself as she rocked her body in time with her Mistress. Cassandra drove in and out, sending waves of pleasure through her with every thrust. She was close now. So close—

Mia cried out as ecstasy burst deep in her core, rippling through her entire body. She arched into Cassandra, toes and fingers curling, arms pulling against her restraints. Cassandra's thrusts were unrelenting, drawing her orgasm on and on until it dissolved into nothing, leaving Mia breathless and spent on the bed.

But as she lay back, her eyes closed, her body boneless and weak, Cassandra's fingers trailed up the side of her neck.

"Oh, we're not done yet." She leaned down, her breath tickling Mia's ear. "You got what you wanted. Now it's my turn."

Hmm? Mia peered up at her Mistress. Why did she have such a wicked look in her eyes? And why was she taking off the strap-on?

Cassandra pulled it down her legs and tossed it aside,

then climbed on top of Mia again. She could feel Cassandra's wetness at the base of her stomach, could feel the warmth between her legs. Mia longed to touch her, feel her quiver under her fingertips, give her Mistress the same release that she'd given her. But tied to the bed, her wrists bound, she was powerless to do anything at all.

"Mistress," she begged. "May I touch you? May I please you?"

Cassandra skimmed a finger over Mia's breasts, circling a nipple with her fingertip. "Oh, don't you worry. I intend for you to do just that."

She shifted up the bed toward the headboard. Mia trembled with anticipation. But it wasn't until Cassandra's knees were at either side of Mia's shoulders that she realized her Mistress had no intention of untying her hands.

"I may have allowed you some freedom tonight," Cassandra said, "but I still expect you to remember your place. You belong to me. And I expect nothing less than your complete devotion."

"Yes, Mistress," she said softly. "I'm yours to command."

"I only have one command for you tonight." Cassandra grabbed hold of the headboard with both hands. "I want you to *taste me.*"

Slowly, she lowered her hips until she hovered an inch above Mia's head. Straining against her bonds, Mia rose to meet her, her lips brushing against Cassandra's silken folds.

She ran her tongue up and down them, her Mistress's heady scent flooding her senses. She'd never done this with Cassandra before. The taste of her arousal, the feel of her under Mia's lips and tongue—it was intoxicating.

Was this what *she* tasted like? Was she this warm and wet every time her Mistress touched her?

Cassandra let out a pleasured murmur, her hips sinking lower. "That's it. Don't stop."

Mia glided her tongue down to Cassandra's entrance, dipping it inside before snaking it up to her tiny, hooded clit. It was hard and swollen under Mia's tongue. As she strummed it gently, pursed her lips around it, Cassandra's whole body shivered, a moan erupting from her.

"Yes, right there," she said. "Faster."

Mia obeyed, licking and sucking and swirling, relishing every tremor, every gasp. All the while, Cassandra rocked and ground her hips, pushing back against Mia's mouth.

And slowly, her moans grew louder. Slowly, her movements became more frantic.

Slowly, she came undone.

"Yes!" Cassandra's hand fell to Mia's head, gripping her hair tightly. "Yes—"

Her thighs locked around Mia's ears, her head tipping back as an orgasm took her. Her cry echoed through the room and her body quaked, shaking the bed beneath them. She held onto Mia's hair with clenched fists as she rode out her climax, until finally, her body stilled.

She collapsed onto the bed beside Mia, her chest heaving with heavy breaths. But that didn't stop her from pulling Mia's face toward hers in a greedy, possessive kiss.

Mia murmured into her lips. "Thank you, Mistress."

Cassandra broke away, untying Mia's wrists with practiced hands before sweeping her into her arms. Mia closed her eyes, dissolving into her Mistress's sweet embrace.

But Cassandra wasn't just her Mistress, not anymore.

And Mia wasn't just her submissive. She wasn't her lover, or her girlfriend, either. She was all those things, and so much more.

Now, Mia truly belonged to her, body and mind, soul and heart.

EPILOGUE

"Riley," Cassandra called. "Can you give us a hand?"

Riley joined her and Ava by the mirror. "What do you need?"

"Just hold up her hair while I zip up her dress." Cassandra looked around the room. "And where is Penelope? The wedding planner was looking for her. There's a problem with the heating. The guests are going to freeze in this weather—"

"Cass, stop." Ava turned to face her. "You're not supposed to be doing any of this. You're not supposed to be doing anything at all."

"I can't just sit around. I need to make sure everything goes smoothly."

"No, you don't. That's not your job today. Because if there's one day you can let someone else take the reins, it's your wedding day." She put her hands on Cassandra's shoulders. "Relax. Stop trying to do everything yourself. Take it from me. Once I stopped worrying and trusted my maid of honor to take care of things, I was able to enjoy my wedding far more. So why don't you let *your* maid of honor return the favor?"

"But—"

"I'm finished getting dressed. I'll go find the wedding planner. Just stay here and get ready. I'm sure Riley can handle getting you into your dress."

The sudden panic that flashed in Riley's eyes suggested otherwise. Nevertheless, they gave Cassandra a nod. "I got this."

"I'll be right back." With that, Ava disappeared from the room.

"Looks like it's just the two of us," Riley said. "Let's get you into that dress."

With a little help from Riley, Cassandra slipped into the long-sleeved, ivory silk gown. As Riley zipped it up, Cassandra adjusted her hair in the mirror. Her curls had been styled half up, half down, a single diamond hairpin adorning them.

Simple but elegant. That was what both she and Mia had wanted for their small winter wedding. But they'd allowed themselves one indulgence—the venue. Most of the guests had no idea what was behind the black doors of Casa de la Diosa. However, Cassandra and Mia planned to make full use of those rooms during their honeymoon.

"There," Riley said. "You're good to go."

Cassandra turned to face them. "How do I look?"

"You look beautiful." Riley gave her a small smile. "I'm really happy for you, Cass. And for Mia. You two deserve this. You deserve a lifetime of happiness."

"Thank you." She pulled Riley into a firm embrace, grateful that they allowed her the indulgence, just this once.

There was a knock on the door. A moment later, Ava slipped into the room. "I spoke to the planner. She found Penelope and they sorted out the heating. Everything is fine. We're ahead of schedule."

Cassandra breathed a sigh of relief. "Thank you."

"You look beautiful, by the way." Ava smiled. "I can't believe you're getting married."

"Honestly? Neither can I." Cassandra turned to the window. Outside, the guests were making their way to the snowy glade behind the chateau where the ceremony would take place. "If you'd told me years ago that I'd be standing before that altar, saying my vows to the woman of my dreams? I wouldn't have believed it. Yet here I am. And I wouldn't trade it for anything in the world."

Ava joined her by the window, taking both Cassandra's hands in hers. "Treasure that feeling. And enjoy this day, because you only get one. But this is just the beginning. It only gets better from here."

"You say that, but you've barely been married a year," Cassandra said.

"Yes, and every day has been better than the last."

There was another knock on the door. "It's Penelope. All the guests are seated. Everything is in place. You can start as soon as you're ready."

Cassandra took a deep breath. "Let's get going."

Picking up the skirt of her dress, she left the room, Riley ahead of her and Ava behind her. They made their way through the chateau's hallways until they reached the back doors.

Cassandra stepped outside and headed down the short path to the glade, which had been cleared of snow and transformed for an open-air ceremony. The altar was positioned at the edge of the bluff before a backdrop of the surrounding mountain ranges.

Her arrival was the signal for the wedding to begin. As the small string quartet began to play and the guests rose to their feet, Cassandra made her way up the aisle, followed by the small wedding party. Cassandra's was made up of Ava and Riley, while Mia's party was her mother and her sister Holly, along with Tess, who she'd become fast friends with.

They joined Cassandra by the altar. Then came the moment she'd been waiting for.

There. Mia appeared at the end of the aisle, radiant in a white lace gown and a fur-lined cape, her hair a copper crown against a backdrop of white, adorned with tiny flowers.

Cassandra watched, breathless, as she glided up the aisle, bouquet in hand. The woman walking toward her? She wasn't the girl who had stood before Cassandra the night they met, hesitant and uncertain.

No, she was the woman Cassandra had seen in the mirror that night right before they made love for the first time. A woman so beautiful, confident, passionate that Cassandra hadn't been able to resist her. A woman who deserved all the love in the world and had so graciously allowed Cassandra to give her that love, along with the gift of her vulnerability.

A woman who had transformed Cassandra's world, her heart.

Mia stopped before her, her cheeks the same shade of pink as her lips, and gave her a demure smile. And just like that night in the chateau, the rest of the world faded away and it was just the two of them, standing together at the altar, lost in each other.

Cassandra barely heard a word of the officiant's speech. She barely heard a word of her vows, or Mia's. But she felt them, deep in her heart. And when the officiant pronounced them married, her soul soared up past the mountains and into the heavens.

And after they exchanged their first kiss, Cassandra took her wife's hands in hers and whispered into her ear.

"Mia," she said. "*Mine.*"

ABOUT THE AUTHOR

Anna Stone is the author of lesbian romance bestsellers Being Hers, Tangled Vows, and more. Her sizzling sapphic romances feature strong, passionate women who love women. In every one of her books, you'll find off-the-charts heat and a guaranteed happily ever after.
Anna lives in Australia with her girlfriend and their cat. When she isn't writing, she can usually be found with a coffee in one hand and a book in the other.

Visit **annastoneauthor.com** to find out more about her books and to sign up for her newsletter.

Printed in Great Britain
by Amazon